AFG ✗

EAVES LANE

-2 MAR 1979   13. FEB. 1980

27 MAR 1979

                    -1. REC JUL80   -17. NOV 1982
                    -1. JUL 1980

-3. APR. 1979   ECCLESTON
                                16. MAY 1984

16. JUL 1979   20. JUN. 1984
            19 AUG 1980

                    27 MAY 1980   27. JUN. 1984

11. SEP 1979   CHORLEY

                                IDL from CC.
            10-4 NOV 1980   To .... PP

16. MAY 1979   -4. NOV. 1980   Due 25/4/91
                17. NOV. 1980

15 DEC 1979

                18. SEP. 1981   13. APR 91
                                01. SEP 92

THE DARK JOURNEY

Diana Raymond

*

THE DARK JOURNEY

CASSELL
LONDON

CASSELL LTD.
35 Red Lion Square, London WC1R 4SG
and at Sydney, Auckland, Toronto, Johannesburg,
an affiliate of
Macmillan Publishing Co., Inc.,
New York.

First published 1978

ISBN 0 304 30236 8

Typeset by Inforum Ltd, Portsmouth.
Printed and bound in Great Britain by
Billing and Sons Ltd., Guildford.

FOR ERNEST

and that large company who
have gone, taking our love
with them

The country's nearer now,
That place which in childhood seemed
Far, forgotten, not even with the substance
Of things dreamed.

They were here once:
Their voices and their laughter filled
The rooms of life with purpose and with love —
These now are stilled.

That other country knows
Some essence of their being and their mind —
Unknown, unheard; yet at moments catching
The ear like wind.

For now the world of time
Is built no more of certainty and stone,
But holds within its structure and its pace
Those deeps unknown.

Here there is silence.
Here one goes by street and hill and shore
Without them, knowing that touch and voice
Can ease no more.

Yet still we question,
Still turn towards the shadowed distant place,
Straining to know, to hear; to see
The transfigured face.

1

Eve wrote, on the clear foolscap page, amongst the other words: 'We talk to each other, we say acceptable things; then we go home and throw ourselves out of the window.'

§

The voice, it seemed, had been pursuing her for some time. She stood still in the London street, in the full sunlight.

'I say! *Do* wait a minute!'

Puzzled, Eve looked over her shoulder. Traffic passed, dazzling and noisy in the warm day.

'*There* you are! I've been running after you for ages.'

Indeed, the woman who came up to her was breathless: large, too warmly dressed, she wasn't built for running. Her face, round but middle-aged, was flushed and damp with sweat. A straw hat slid askew. She carried a plastic bag which she offered in triumph.

'I think this must be *yours*. Just now in the bookshop . . . you put it down while you looked at the books. And I put down my carrier bag, and when I looked for it, mine had gone and yours was left . . . That's what happened, wasn't it? Of course it was a mistake.'

Eve looked at the woman with placid incomprehension. The flushed face with escaping fair hair made no sense.

'You *have* got it, haven't you?' the woman said. 'That green carrier bag? . . . I'd just bought my husband a shirt and things, and when I looked in here there was a loaf and some cheese . . . Well, you can see; it's not the same thing at all.'

Eve said, 'No.'

The pink face lost some of its buoyancy. 'I know it was a mistake, but if I went home and gave my husband bread and cheese when he was expecting a shirt — it wouldn't do, would it?'

'No, I suppose not.'

They exchanged carrier bags; the woman looked into her own, exclaiming, 'Yes, *that's* it: shirt and socks and everything.'

1

Eve made an effort. 'I'm very sorry. I wasn't thinking——'

'No, of course not.' The face now showed little but a desire to be gone. 'So easy to do — though the carriers aren't a bit alike — but when one's mind's on other things . . .'

'I'm very sorry,' she repeated, 'to have given you all this trouble.' Beyond that, Eve could think of nothing to say.

'It doesn't matter at all. Now I've got it back. In these days, the idea of *losing* . . .' She turned to go; turned again. 'There's nothing the matter, is there?'

'No.'

'You're quite all right?'

'Oh yes, thank you.'

'You've gone rather a funny colour.'

'I'm afraid I always look like that.'

'I'll be off then!'

With infinite gladness, it seemed, she strode away on sturdy legs, carrying the shirt and socks for the husband who awaited her.

Eve looked at the bag in her hand as if she hadn't seen it before. Stupid to have taken the other one; could have landed her in trouble: a kind of shop-lifting. She moved among the crowd, making her way home.

The house looked on to Marsham Square, just far enough from Pimlico to be called Chelsea; trees were alive with new green, and tulip, lilac and iris decorated the flower beds with the colours of illuminated manuscript. The houses, with tall porticoes, were divided into flats. Eve climbed the stairs (carpeted but shabby), put her key in the lock, opened and closed the door. So commonplace a ritual, but now it was marked upon her mind with the small shadow of dread. Sunlight showed a dust on wooden surfaces; the air smelled warm, a little stale.

She opened a window, and the voices of children, high-pitched, formless and cheerful, drifted in with the air. Saturday, of course: the odd, blank day, for some reason worse when the weather was fine. Within the rooms silence pressed upon her ears: the silence seemed more than itself, like the quality of air at a great height when breathing became hard.

She would not think about height.

At the back of her mind, beyond the silence, was an echo of many voices, lamentation, even laughter, but these now were quiet. The telephone was silent. She picked up letters from the floor; one from her solicitor (she would wait before opening that); advertisements, pleas for charity; a holiday brochure flying bright emblems of Greece, Spain and Yugoslavia; some were addressed to Jamie himself. She left them where they lay, for everything could wait.

She stood by the window: red tulips burned through the day and the dazzle of May green shifted in wind-driven light. Of this she had no part.

The summons of the door-bell reached her like sound through sleep. When it rang a second time she made herself answer it.

'Hullo, it's me!' The smile on the young woman's face forcedly cheerful. She lived in the flat below, had four children under seven and a husband who was an engineer. She held out a plate. 'I was cooking and thought you might like this.' Good brown eyes, contrasting fair hair that fell to her shoulders; tall, slim, wearing blue belted trousers and a shirt that showed young breasts. Pretty, concerned with life, yet with time to do this. 'Hope it's all right: steak and kidney . . . No, I won't come in, thanks all the same: they're waiting to be fed — John as well.' John was her husband.

'Yes, of course. It's awfully kind of you.'

'Not a bit.' Calm, unflustered, unlike the woman in the street. Eve took the pie, home-made with fluted crust, and put it on the small dining-table. It spoke of kindness, of that peripheral care which could not touch the centre. For a while she followed John's wife, Claudia, in her mind, as she returned to the lively flat below, to the chaos and the welcome, to the happy and demanding day. Then she lost her.

Having no inclination to eat, she sat and looked at the pie.

It was not yet one o'clock: the day had a long way to go. She went again to the window, for though she had no part of the colour and warmth and sound out there, the traffic of people and cars spoke of places beyond the isolation of these walls, the isolation in her own head.

Not yet one o'clock. Five hours till evening; another four till night. She stood unmoving, tracing it back, going through it all once more. 'But you have a *future*, Mrs Rutherford!' some woman had exclaimed.

It did not seem so.

§

3

She could not now remember what had kept her within doors on that other day. For mountain addicts the weather had been promising enough, with early cloud breaking to throw cloaks of light on the Borrowdale fells. Not much wind; the hall of the hotel full of voices and plans, ropes, boots and rucksacks. A man and his wife tracing a path on the wall map: 'If we leave the car here below Manesty, we can make a circle . . .'

Jamie, her husband, said, 'You're not coming? You've quite decided?'

She said Yes; she was taking a day off. It had been a small subject of contention; not a full quarrel. Jamie said, 'I shall miss you.'

'No, you won't. If you're doing Merlin's Crack, you'll be glad I'm not there: I always make a nonsense of the chimney, I can never find the hold. And that keeps everyone hanging about, and you hate hanging about.'

He stood before her, large, bearded, brown curling hair touched with grey, eyes blue and alive, skin coloured by open weather: all familiar, as familiar as life.

He said with a small shrug of resignation, 'I'm never glad you're not there.'

For some reason she had given this only passing attention; perhaps another voice had distracted her. Out of the corner of her eye she was aware of Jamie's face, for the words had been serious, not lightly spoken. A small humorous enquiry in his glance impressed itself on her, even while she caught other words, talk of the climb, someone mentioning her name.

'No,' she called, 'I'm not coming — I'll have lunch in.'

Jamie had then turned away; he was already discussing some aspect of the climb, her failure to answer, it seemed, forgotten. She followed him into the drive. Here were the cars, their boots open to receive the paraphernalia of climbing; the cool morning air, jokes, plans, the watching headlands patched with light, the walls of the farmhouse across the way brilliant as snow.

David and Sarah Murray, who were climbing with Jamie, slung their sacks into the car; Sarah lingered to talk with Eve. 'Should be fun,' Sarah said. She was thirty, but looked younger, and seemed to be built on springs. Dark hair cut very short: she said once, 'I look like a stunted Henry the Fifth.' David, her husband, was tall and fair, lazy-voiced: 'a marvellous man on the rope,' Jamie called him; 'even when he swears — as all climbers do — it sounds like a blessing. Sarah's the one who explodes; when

4

she gets stuck on a pitch the air turns blue.'

Sarah said now, 'Why don't you come? No sex equality, with two chaps and me.'

Eve shook her head. 'Taking a day off.' No need to recount the argument, her own obstinate resistance. Sarah never took a day off, but Sarah was more than ten years younger. Eve went on, 'I'll walk a bit, write a letter to Nigel: ought to have written yesterday.'

'Mm . . . must be kind of nice to have a son,' Sarah said. Eve looked at her as she dug with one booted foot at the gravel. Hard to remember that two years ago Sarah's own son had been still-born; hard to see Sarah in the context of failure.

Eve stopped herself from saying, 'You've plenty of time.' 'Yes, it's good to have a son. I just wish——'

Sarah's small amused face turned to her. 'Oh, there's always *something* one just wishes . . .'

Jamie called, 'We want to climb before dark — anyone put my lunch in?'

Sarah went bounding off, as most people did when Jamie called them. Could I be jealous of her? Eve wondered as Jamie flung an affectionate arm round Sarah's shoulders; but thought not, because after nearly twenty years of marriage she no longer looked on him as a separate person but as part of herself. A part with whom she could quarrel, of course, and fight even, but who built her universe about her.

('I feel a part of you,' she had said, and he answered, 'Well, just at the moment, you are'; but she had smiled and held him more closely, and not answered because it wasn't only love-making she meant, good though that was: she wanted to say, I'm built into you; you make me angry sometimes, and I suppose I resent the fact that I do mostly what *you* want, but I can't imagine anything without you, not a walk in the rain, nor streets, nor tube-stations, nor even a heavy cold, because even if you were absent, you'd be somewhere in my head, making sense of it all . . .

Later he said, 'You're beautiful . . . maybe a bit too beautiful: who was that tedious guy with a white moustache beside you at dinner? He was letting his soup go cold staring down your neck.'

She laughed and turned in bed, putting her head in the pillow. 'I don't know who he was, except that he dealt in houses.'

'He dealt in beautiful women, who've no right to be lovely at forty. Did he make any passes?'

'Not beyond routine.'

'And what the hell does that mean?'

She was still smiling, muffled by the pillow. 'I like it when chaps make passes and you get cross.'

'Oh, fine, fine. Isn't that absolutely fine.'

'You know what I mean.'

'Not sure.'

'Yes, you do. Because I don't want anything but you, and you make most of the running. Jamie Rutherford, well-known climber, paints too: profile of Jamie Rutherford, interview with Jamie Rutherford . . . but you mind when boring old men of sixty put their hands on my knee . . .'

'I thought so——'

'It's the only thing I've got; it's something to hold over you.'

'Oh, you extraordinary girl. You don't need to hold anything over me; you know *that* after twenty years, and if you don't, you ought to have your head examined.'

After a silence she said, 'Is that true?'

He'd gone to sleep.

'What true?'

'What you just said.'

'Everything I've just said is true.')

No, she wasn't jealous. Bloody lucky, she thought, because I could be: young things in tight jeans come and ask him about the Himalayas: it'd be all too easy because Jamie, even nearing fifty, has all the charm in the world, and that exuberant friendliness which can jar so much when it's untrue, and warm so much when it's real, as it is with him. And I've never been the kind to be *sure*: not to be sure of anything, certainly not myself. Beautiful, he said; but you can't be certain — there's this face which you have with you all the time, and sometimes it looks good, and sometimes it looks terrible, and I couldn't know less about the right kind of clothes: I like slacks and sweaters and old shoes. I can remember having spots when I was young, so badly that I didn't want to go out: that was when I was fifteen, just after Father took off for America and never came back, never even wrote, and poor Ma went into a kind of mental decline (financial too), so I'd nothing to offer when girls at school talked about their parents. ('Father's a doctor and Mother makes the most marvellous cakes she could have been an actress she went to drama school but she had to give it up when she married and had all of us . . .') No, as an only child she had nothing to offer. ('Is *that* your mother? Why does she wear those funny clothes? Why does she talk to herself?') And Jamie could sometimes be angry with her, for she was careless in memory; could forget important messages, muddle the time of a meeting, muddle the hold on a climb . . . Not possible, ever, to be sure.

Yet at some depth which she couldn't explore or explain, Jamie was a certainty: his love was woven into the fabric of existence, a large assurance which more often than not she took for granted . . . how much time had to pass before you learned *not* to take the good things for granted?

She stood and watched as they all got into the car. Jamie was driving; before he folded himself into the seat he waved to her. 'Good climbing!' she called, waving back, wishing to repair at this late moment some small failure. But Merlin's Crack in Gillercombe, though hard, wasn't a long climb; they'd be home by tea-time, talking of pitches and belays and overhangs, absorbed as all experts are, as if nothing beyond the rock and surmounting it was of importance.

She watched them go.

The car sent up a little flurry of grit; Sarah waved from the back seat. The sight of them remained with her as she went indoors.

The hotel was quieter now.

At the reception desk the young plump secretary tapped evenly on her typewriter. One of the waiters, dark, Italian, lingered to talk to the secretary, who laid down her typewriter and took up her charm. The odd-job man came and made an unwelcome third by discussing a blocked pipe. Two elderly women, one with a stick, moved slowly through the hall, talking together. Would they perhaps go for a walk, or might it rain; luncheon was at one ʼclock; they could perhaps have coffee and biscuits, a glass of sherry at twelve.

No reason why these exchanges — as they did — should shadow her; old age was still a long way off, another country. She settled herself at a table in the living-room. The room, its empti-ness emphasised by squares of emerging sunlight on the carpet, spoke of those who were already on the move, rucksacks slung, up the first of the mountain paths, perhaps towards Gable or the Pike. The local bus which ran the six miles to Keswick made its punctual brisk passing, a red gleam beyond the garden's edge.

She began the letter to her son.

'Darling Nigel — It looks like a fine day, but I'm being lazy and taking time off. I hope you're enjoying yourself with Mark...'

She looked at these words on the page. In one sense, of course, they were not true. Briefly, the small insincerities of all communication oppressed her. She looked unseeingly ahead, as if Nigel stood there in reproach.

Sixteen years old, growing tall, brown curling hair and wide-spaced blue eyes like his father's; the mouth full, occasionally sulky, more often wide with laughter, showing the splendid white teeth of the young.

Sixteen. Not a child any more, as Jamie often reminded her; already with his secret interests and desires. As it should be, of course: large in her mind were the instructions for mothers to Let Them Go; Not Interfere; that Birds must Fly the Nest.

Jamie had no difficulty with all this: when Nigel had opted to stay with Mark on the Easter holiday he'd shrugged and said, 'Why not?'

'But he *likes* the mountains——'

'Not sure.' Jamie was mending an electric plug: his hands square, not beautiful, worked with care. 'I've sometimes thought he comes along just to please.'

She had protested: she could see Nigel following his father over the wide shoulder of Green Gable or Allen Crags; she could see him with the rope about his waist, at the foot of the Easy or Moderate climbs Jamie had chosen for him. She tried to put away the moments when Nigel had failed to find his foothold, and Jamie had shown nothing but patience which revealed to her (and to Nigel, she had no doubt) the impatience beneath.

No more to be said. Nigel went to spend the Easter holiday with his schoolfriend, Mark Stevens; Eve and Jamie went to Borrowdale in Cumbria.

'... a good time with Mark.' She could see Mark Stevens clearly: taller, thin, long-haired, eyes which ran down at the corners; a manner so polite that politeness contained a mockery of itself; a side-glance, the sensation in his presence that when you'd gone he would tilt at you with malice or wit.

Older by six months, more brilliant than Nigel: I don't like him, Eve thought; I've never liked him, from the first time when we all had tea together in the hotel near the school: he ate his muffins and said 'Thank you'; wiped his fingers on a surprisingly clean handkerchief, and conveyed that he held secret knowledge to everyone's disadvantage.

8

So it wasn't quite true to say '. . . a good time with Mark.'

She returned to the letter. She would (she hoped) make him laugh about the young man who set out from the hotel with every possible piece of climbing equipment, brilliant 'ironmongery', a polished nylon rope; then was discovered not a mile away, lying on his back, asleep in the sun. She went on, 'Next time you must come with us — Daddy enjoys taking you up the Moderates as much as he enjoys the Severes——'

That wasn't quite true either.

Unsatisfied she took the letter to the small post office, twenty yards from the hotel. Here she lingered in the sun. The little red letter-box was set in a grey stone wall: she tried to imagine the letter's arrival in the Kentish house, which she had never seen.

Nigel had made efforts to describe the house: she saw something large, pleasing, a garden falling in terraces: perhaps it wasn't like that at all. Mark's parents were faceless too: Nigel had given no clear picture. 'They're all right; his mother's pretty and his father likes boats.' Nothing you could focus on — but then to a boy of sixteen parents inhabited another country, to be seen only through a haze of uninterest.

She wandered along the country road. Here the lower fells and heads, the ridge of Narrow Moor, the point of Castle Crag, were sculptured in light, but if she turned back to look westward, the higher peaks were dark with rising cloud. Hands in the pockets of her trousers, she stood looking towards the cloud. Familiar: so many times she had seen the spread of grey lift like a shaken sediment, and shadow the tops which clustered above Stye Head. It would be sunless on the climb, where Jamie, David and Sarah must now be on the rock face. Where she stood the sun endured: the day was divided. Indeed the iron-dark clouds over there to the west emphasised the brilliance and warmth in this part of the valley.

Beguiled by the sun, she crossed the bridge over the beck and began lazily to climb the Watendlath path, but the massing clouds swarmed quickly; soon there was only a little shore of light on the far end of Derwentwater, towards Keswick. Rock and heather had a brightness of their own, though the sky was now wholly covered, purple in the west, the colour of blackberry juice. A stronger wind rose, hunting through the rough grass, whipping at her hair; larch trees and hazel bushes bent, like runners bringing news.

9

With the strengthening wind, she felt the first flick of rain. How far were they on the climb? She returned to the hotel, with the day darkening all the time and the rain increasing. This would do nothing to halt Jamie; rough weather hardened his determination; he even welcomed it. As the wild day strengthened, she thought of Jamie's relish for the difficult things, the joyous acceptance of adversity. Something in this, perhaps, of pride: the only son of a parson father and an over-anxious mother, he had been alternately disciplined and cherished. During the war, his school had been evacuated to North Wales; there he had begun to climb. Protests from his mother; protests of a different kind from his father: 'A waste of time: your report suggests that you have a good brain, but art and mountaineering won't make a career for a man, and as you must know a parson doesn't leave much to his son.'

This, no more than weather, had deterred Jamie from climbing; politely but stubbornly he had continued, finding early that passion for the rocks and the summits which like all loves goes beyond reason.

Determination, the lack of — or control of — fear had taken him to the heights in more ways than one: combined with moderate fame as a painter, gradually earned, he came to the front of that band of climbers whose names and photographs find place in the newspapers and on the television screen.

This now sunless day with the wind-driven rain would not deflect him, and Sarah and David would follow, because those who were with Jamie did what he wanted. They would return, anoraks shiny with wet, faces whipped and coloured by wind and rain, voices frayed from calling against the weather's sound, thirsty, triumphant. She looked out at the rain which drove across the fell-sides. Wet and cold on the rocks, but now she wished she was there; she had absorbed enough of Jamie's philosophy to feel relish for adversity.

Some walkers returned, having abandoned the day, their clothes and faces dripping like sponge; ('Wet clothing will be collected at seven' the ominous notice read.) A man, mopping his face with a useless handkerchief, asked what her husband was doing, and she said, 'Merlin's Crack.' 'Rather him than me,' he said. 'Give me the fire and an afternoon snooze. I like my rocks warm.'

There was indeed a fire in the sitting-room: the logs spat, and an auburn long-haired retriever lay asleep before it; every now and again his ear twitched with some stimulant of his dream. The drenching day and the cold rocks seemed far off. Yet the pitches of the climb came clear to her, the steep gullies and chimney, carved in the mountain so long ago by the ancient ice.

After luncheon, Eve went up to their room. Her dressing-gown lay flung over a chair, her slippers askew: absently she tidied these because Jamie could when tired become exasperated by untidiness; combed her hair before the looking-glass. This showed the tireless rain at the window behind her, and the dusky image of her face. Straight dark hair, the eyes grey-green, the mouth full, the skin clear and pale. Though she could become helpless with laughter, the face in repose had a mark of sadness, which could not surely be justified. Yes, all right, she thought: a good enough face, I suppose. It'll do for a while longer. She could see a likeness to Nigel, and this she found disturbing, as if the legacy of bone and flesh had been like some act too carelessly performed.

Absurd, of course; simply that this day of darkening rain made her regret his absence.

The afternoon was quiet. She read by the fire, dozed for a few minutes, tired by yesterday's climb. When she opened her eyes the air beyond the windows had the colour of slate; cloud obscured entirely the western hills.

A distant rattle of tea-cups. Sleepy still, she thought the sound carried reassurance: at the back of her mind was an old, perhaps not even true, memory of rainy afternoons when the fire spat and tea came as celebration, with toasted crumpets and chocolate cake . . .

Now she sat turned towards the door. Soon they'd be home, drenched, tired and talkative. Now she remembered his words: *I'm never glad you're not there*; and she thought she could echo them: this was an empty time, waiting for him. By twos and threes the parties returned; voices filled the room, names of heights and climbs wove a pattern of sound, with the treble of tea-cups. The dog roused himself and wandered about the room, getting in the way. Eve said to a tall man of about sixty who wore shorts and was standing with his cup of tea and cake balanced dangerously together, 'Did you see my husband and the others on Merlin's Crack?' He shook his head and said with his mouth full: 'Couldn't see a damn thing, dear lady. Mist from the top of Stye Head. Not a view in a bucket-load; certainly not from the summit of Gable. That's why we turned home. Damn silly business, climbing three

11

thousand feet in cotton-wool.'

Mist would make small difference to the climb: the hand and footholds would be clear enough. Though the leader would be out of sight, his voice would carry . . .

But it would take longer, of course.

Someone turned on the light, which made the weather outside a darker grey. The sound of voices thinned as the climbers finished their tea and went upstairs to bath and change. The tall man lay back in a chair, empty cup and plate beside him. 'Suppose I should go too, but having climbed up Stye Head, I balk at the staircase.'

'You're sure you didn't see them?'

'See who?'

'My husband and his friends.'

'Oh . . . sorry. Bit sleepy, what with the fire and the buns. You mean on Merlin's Crack. Saw them setting off; not after that. Lost to sight like everything else. I told you.'

Lost to sight. The words had overtones: *I watched them for a long time through the telescope until they were lost to sight.* Perhaps she hadn't quite got the words; they seemed to belong to legend. The last sight of Mallory and Irvine? Perhaps. Another world of climbing: the tremendous icy skirts of Everest, the elaborate and costly expedition; the unending face of a mountain five miles high.

Not like the brief climbs of these native hills; nothing at all like. Yet, of course, you had only to read the annals of the Rescue Team to know that accidents could happen: these hills, though not high, were dangerous. Dangerous to inexperienced climbers — those who took risks, who didn't prepare for weather or the sudden precipice; not men like Jamie who had climbed, it seemed to her, almost everywhere in the world: the Himalayas, the Alps, the Pyrenees.

The tall man put both hands on the arms of his chair and with a grunt thrust himself to his feet. 'Got to make the effort some time. Stiff in the shanks, but can't expect anything else at my age . . .'

When he'd gone, the room was empty, except for the dog. The rain seemed to drive more heavily, and she felt the first twinge of anger: silly to stay out so long on a day like this; they'd be soaked, and all the baths taken when they returned . . .

It was possible of course that on the easier way home, perhaps by Taylor's Gill Force, or Sour Milk Gill, one of them had slipped, twisted a knee or an ankle. It so often happened, when the tension and care of the climb itself were done, fatigue made you careless on the rough path to the valley. Especially on wet rock.

They might have stopped for tea at one of the cottages in Seathwaite (though would not Jamie have telephoned her?)

Perhaps they had decided against Merlin's Crack (very possible in this weather) and driven to another valley — over Honister to Buttermere, say, and climbed in Burtness Coombe...

With a preliminary cough, the grandfather clock struck the hour. Six o'clock was not after all very late: she had expected them home by four, but the weather would have delayed them, and some other small accident beside.

Guests began to return to the room, having bathed and changed. Chatter about her now; its irrelevance irked her, and she moved away into the reception hall, where the first smells of dinner intruded from the kitchen. A lull fell upon the place, that droop at the end of the day, before the mild festivity of the evening.

After six. She would go upstairs, wash and change; then she'd hear the noise of their return: the car in the drive; steps on the stairs: Jamie's voice, that unmistakable voice; she could even tell his cough.

She began to climb the stairs. The sound of a car stopped her ... Why, they were here! When waiting ended, the time of waiting dissolved; the day turned to normal again in an instant.

She stood still. Through the wide windows she could see Sarah, coming towards the hotel, alone, head down, in the rain.

§

This was the first moment when memory broke. That sight of Sarah, bedraggled, soaked through, coming quickly with her head down stopped her train of thought, for in the few moments as she ran to meet Sarah, nothing had been said, nothing truly known.

After that, the nightmare began. The nightmare was vivid but fragmentary: she could remember feeling sick as she sat in the car beside Sarah but had no tears. There was rain on Sarah's face, and she was shivering; her windcheater, jeans and boots soaked and muddy; there was blood on her hand.

Even though the nightmare had begun, the full darkness hadn't

13

come down: she was afraid, her mouth and throat dry as if they'd been sand-papered, but finality was some way off. Sarah drove fast along the winding valley road. At a great distance was the quiet room in the hotel with the shuffle of the fire, and the little punctuation of the clock: the dull, easy day.

Here was a new thing, frightening as a precipice to an unroped climber; yet not quite true, not quite believable. For this was the familiar road into Keswick, travelled so many hundred times — yet quite changed: the meadows shone emerald with wet, the cattle moved and stared and the fellsides took transient wings of light from the changing day. Familiar, peaceful; but as if some malicious force had shifted its perspective into evil.

Not many words passed between them.

Eve said — 'I don't understand *how* he could have fallen.'

'It was after the chimney. The flake came away; I suppose the wet had loosened it——'

'But he's climbed everywhere; there's nothing he doesn't know about——'

Sarah was silent, miserable, driving fast. In the end she said, 'It was a bad day.'

'He should have turned back.'

'It was all right to start with.'

'Why did you let him go in the ambulance with David? Why didn't you fetch me?'

Sarah still looked miserable. 'David seemed to think — that he should go there quickly.'

'Was he conscious?'

'No.'

Blank road, turn and twist of the car: strengthening light on drenched malevolent green; walkers on the footpath, pushing back the hoods of their anoraks. 'I know the hospital: we went there once years ago when Jamie — had to have stitches in his leg. It was all right; only a deep cut; he had to rest, of course, which he hated——' She became aware of her voice which seemed to be cantering on out of control. 'I don't understand how it happened. I don't understand.'

'It was — one of those things. He couldn't know——'

'I don't understand about the flake——'

'It just came away. Right away. It looked solid, it'd been there for hundreds, I don't know, maybe thousands, of years.'

'I can't remember the flake.'

14

'It was above the chimney, a kind of overhang. A bit airy, exposed. David always said it was difficult, but he hadn't any doubt about Jamie.'

'Couldn't David hold him?'

'He — he fell the length of the rope. David tried, he was belayed himself, but . . .'

On past the sheen of the lake, the skies clearing all the time so the head of Skiddaw before them wore only the suggestion of cloud like a puff of smoke, and made its imprint, lit by the ochre of evening sun, on the still water.

'How long did it take to get the rescue people?'

'David went down to Seathwaite and raised the alarm. I — I stayed with Jamie. The rescue team came with their Land Rover and all the first-aid gear. They had to climb up to us . . . I suppose it took about an hour, perhaps less.'

'I don't understand why no one told me——'

'David had to wait for them, take them to the exact place——'

'He could have telephoned me!'

'He thought . . . I don't know what he thought. I only know when he came back with the rescue boys, he told me to go and get you.'

'Was Jamie conscious at all?'

'No, I don't think so. I think the stone caught his head as he fell.'

'Then he wouldn't've known me. But I want to be with him; oh please, I want to be with him.'

'I know. We're getting there fast.'

Eve sat silent. 'You don't think it's any good.'

'I don't think anything; I don't know. Truly, I don't know. I just know they're taking him to the hospital and David said I was to bring you as quickly as I could.'

'Why didn't I go on the climb?'

A brief glance from Sarah. 'It wouldn't've made any difference; it isn't any good, to think like that.'

'I'm not thinking anything: I just . . .' She fell silent.

Sarah said, 'He . . . he couldn't have known what happened: not pain, I mean.'

'You can't be sure of that; he must have felt the fall; he must have felt . . .' They had passed the head of the lake; here was the town.

Everything built of fear: men and women in the streets, shop fronts with anoraks and postcards, all built of fear.

The hospital. Small, nothing extraordinary; broad steps, flower beds. Sarah beside her, one arm round her waist. Something inside her said, 'Here we go.' A time for courage: she had none, only the power to walk on, towards the dark.

§

Memory broke again there. Even then it was still possible for life to go on, it was still possible to hope. While Sarah spoke to the young woman at the reception desk, while they walked together to the ward, the thing wasn't there yet. If she could go back to that moment, there was still much to come. A nurse in passing glanced at her face. Odd that one could move one leg in front of the other when they seemed to be made of straw.

Not conscious, Sarah had said. (What was it like, to fall? 'You can't tell me; oh darling, if you can't tell me, I shan't ever know.') There would be nothing, no words to be spoken, nothing exchanged: an impassable wall. A voice just reaching her: 'I'm afraid, Mrs Rutherford, we've done all we can. . . If you'd like to see him, you'd better come now.'

She stood, held in the silence of fear.

'Would you like to see him?'

'Yes, please.'

'You're quite sure?'

Better to have said No: something one didn't want to remember. Something that would return in the small hours, by harsh and unlovely day: not Jamie at all, a wounded figure, bloodstained and drained of blood, drained almost of life. The sound of breathing heavy like the sound of a machine that will soon be quiet. Frozen, she stood, not knowing how long, listening to the only voice Jamie had now. At last one sudden breath, a sudden lift and turn of his head, then a fall, away from her, away from life.

So this was it. What had had warmth and life and love so short a while ago, now was nothing: this was the last goodbye; this was death.

It can't be true. It can't be happening. They are all coming back to the hotel, late for tea, and the day will go on. The evening will go on, as all the evenings have, and there is a long time, a long long time of weeks and months and years, because we are still quite young. . .

No, there is no more time.

'You'd better come back to the hotel.'

Sarah, perhaps.

Yes, Sarah beside her.

'You'd better come back, love,' Sarah said. 'You look terrible.'

'I don't think——'

'There isn't any more to do here.'

'No.'

Sarah's arm round her.

'I think I'm going to be sick.'

'All right: we'll find a place and I'll wait for you.'

She wasn't sick, only cold and frightened. The looking-glass set in white tiles showed a face distorted perhaps by light and colour.

Sarah, gently waiting. Eve said, 'Don't they want to ask me questions? Don't they want——'

'David'll see to that.' Oh yes, David had been there, in the ward. 'Come on, you're coming back with me.'

'To the hotel?'

For a moment the word held comfort: the hotel where she had spent that unknowing idle day, where she had written to Nigel, from where Jamie had gone that morning, with a wave ——

No, it would be quite new: not a place she recognised or understood. She let herself be led to the car, driven back along the darkening road. Eve said, 'I think he'd like . . . would have liked . . . to be buried here.'

'Yes.'

'I suppose he'd have liked that: I don't know. I suppose it doesn't matter: why does one think it matters?'

'It's something you can do.'

'But . . . alone. I mean he won't know.'

'We're here,' Sarah said.

Eve stood in the chill of the drive. Lights shone into the dusk, as if the hotel were a place of welcome. She said, 'I don't want to go into our — my room.' You had to learn, from now on, to say 'my'.

The guests, Sarah told her, were all at dinner; the sitting-room empty. It was quite simple; she had only to walk into the room and sit while Sarah brought her a drink. Someone had put a new log on the fire, and the sound and smell of burning wood mixed with this moment in her mind.

But the room was loud with another voice, another presence which she would neither see nor hear again. Not ever, for the rest of her life.

She said, 'I'm frightened,' but saw that Sarah had left her. She returned with the glass in her hand, and Eve drank obediently, not knowing what she drank. She said, 'This is the same day that began this morning.' She didn't know if the words made sense. She drank further and then said, 'I think this is the easiest part. I mean, for a little while everyone'll be there, just as you are now, giving me things I need, surrounding me.'

'We'll go on doing it.'

'No — you can't. No one can.' Perhaps the liquor had done something to steady her nerve, or clear her mind. 'In a way this is the easiest time. The real time of being without him hasn't begun.'

§

Various words were used: shock, absence, total alteration of life; the mystery of final parting. At first a calm frenzy possessed her, such as afflicts a nervous hostess who has asked too many people to a party on a day when she's sickening for flu. A continual turbulence within her; but it was necessary to speak, arrange, face both the honest condolence and the embarrassed encounter; to give the right answers, cause no trouble, or no more than was inevitable. For of course the sudden death of a man whose name was well enough known to merit notice in the newspapers and on radio and television could not but provoke disturbance, the alteration of plans, like the sudden breakdown of a train on a long journey. Time was altered. And somewhere in all this — perhaps a saving thing — the thread of pride, of importance, that she had won, like a dark medal, the final harsh distinction of loss.

A doubt persisted, at times out-topping all else. She did not know on which side she stood; she only knew what she wanted.

'He's not a child any more,' Sarah said in answer: 'let him make up his own mind.'

'No — that's too difficult. Suppose he decides not to come, then afterwards he might regret it, and turn round and say that I ought to have made him——'

'Nigel's not like that.'

'No one knows what Nigel's like, or will be.'

'You want him to come?'

'Yes, of course, of course.' Most clearly she could see him with her mind's eye — no, with something more: the heart's eye, perhaps. Jamie's son, that mysterious incarnation of marriage, a being with desires and fears of his own, yet owing his existence to Jamie, who was dead, and herself. 'Oh yes, I want to see him: he's all I've got — no, I don't mean that: that sounds full of self-pity, like some woman crying in the street — but I want to see him.'

'Well, that's settled then——'

'No, it isn't; *I* want to see him, but it may not be the best thing for *him*: don't you see?'

'Yes.'

'It *might* not. The finality; seeing the coffin and everything. If he doesn't see all that, perhaps it'd be easier for him. After all — he was away from his father much of the time. If only he were younger or older I could be sure: if he was about seven years old, I'd keep him away; if he was eighteen, he'd come.'

David said he thought Nigel was grown-up for his age.

'Yes — but this is such a big thing. The largest he's ever faced.'

Sarah said, 'Tell him that you want him to come, that you want him here.'

'I don't know. I don't know if that's right.' She had entered a place, it seemed, where decision became marshy ground. 'That puts pressure on him, doesn't it: he couldn't say no——'

'For goodness sake!'

'I know I'm being tiresome. I know I am. I can't help it. It's so important, what happens to Nigel now. What I do. Because he mustn't feel. . .'

'Mustn't feel what?'

'That there's too much weight on him. That *I'm* too much weight on him. He's too young to have that. And yet — oh, God, I want to see him!'

'If he's to be here in time, you'll have to telephone tonight.'

'I know. I know.'

In the end the issue was decided, not by any of them.

Later that evening, in the hour before dinner, with rain freckling the windows, Eve heard the sounds of arrival in the drive.

There was no one with him. He wore a dark blue raincoat, perhaps in deference. She watched him as he got out of the car (a ramshackle Ford which plied between Keswick and the hotel, driven by a young man from Seatoller). He paid the driver without fumbling; he didn't look to be a child, till, as he turned, she caught a glimpse of the smooth-skinned pale face, the light brown hair (Jamie's hair) darkened by rain.

She stood still, recognising a flood of relief, extraordinary, out of all bounds, perhaps something to be afraid of. For instead of the quiet cold unknown figure which had been Jamie as she last saw him, here was his son, walking towards the hotel, flesh and blood, not lost, but here in the breathing world.

Important not to show too much of this. He came into the hall carrying his bag. Perhaps he hadn't expected to see her so soon. 'Hullo, Ma.'

She hugged him. Perfectly possible not to cry. The relief was so extreme that it enabled her to keep control.

He emerged from the embrace, damp hair awry. Young, how young, and yet Jamie there, mysteriously indwelling. Keep to the small facts, her wisdom told her. She said, 'I was going to telephone you this evening.'

'Yes, well, I thought you would. I talked it over with the Stevens——

'It was their idea that you should come?'

His upward glance took in the edge of her question. 'No. I said I wanted to, and Mark's parents said perhaps I should telephone first, but I thought I'd just come. Mark's father drove me to town and I got a train from Euston. He paid my fare, actually, but I told him I'd give it back——'

'Yes, of course: I'll send it to him.' She was glad of these commonplace exchanges.

He stood smoothing his hair. 'I'm terribly sorry about Pa. Has it been awful? I don't understand how he could be killed, just on a climb here in the Lakes.'

He had almost echoed her own words.

'It was . . . we won't talk about it now.' Controlled, still bound in this unfathomable relief. 'We must see about a room — they'll find one for you somewhere.'

The receptionist knew Nigel. She said nicely, 'Terribly sorry about your father, but it's good to see you again. You've grown.'

A little colour came into his face. It had not occurred to her that Nigel was old enough to spark a young woman's coquetry, muffled as it was by condolence, but it occurred to her now. So many new things; had it not been for the towering shadow at her shoulder she could have been diverted by them.

Later she said, 'It's cleared now: come for a walk?'

He nodded, and they wandered out. The sky was clearing, and a flood of yellow-bright, rain-washed sun drove a column of light over the Rosthwaite fells. Below this amongst the cluster of oak and birch, and on the surface of the Stonethwaite beck, evening had come, in moist shadow. The air smelled of pine and streams.

Nigel said, 'What will you do when it's over? I mean——'

'The funeral? Oh, go back home.'

'Would you like me to come too?'

'Oh, yes!' She heard the too fervent cry; said quickly, 'Until you go back to school; it's only a few days.'

'Is it going to be difficult about money?'

'Oh . . . I don't know. I haven't really thought.' (Something that Mark's parents had said? She felt obscurely distressed; such ideas were galloping ahead of her. And whatever reverence the conversation had contained, it was not one she would have wanted to overhear.) 'I shall manage — sell the car, perhaps.' (Jamie's car; maybe she would be glad to be rid of it; it belonged to another life.) She glanced at him with a pang of pity: how large an overturning of his life, from the tranquil holiday in Kent. Did he perhaps fear having to leave Westerfield, his school? Whatever circumstances proved to be, she would make sure that he stayed there. She said as much, and he gave an abstracted nod: 'Oh . . . fine; yes, fine.' Perhaps this wasn't what he had wanted to know . . .

His head was turned towards a crag which lifted above the acid green of drenched grass. 'I remember climbing there once,' he said.

She too gave a glance to the steep rock, greased by lemon light on recent rain. Yes, she too remembered climbing there: Shepherd's Crag, one of the climbs on which Jamie had taken Nigel, perhaps two years ago. For a moment the memory seemed harmless, then it stung, sharp as spirit on a new wound. She would not climb with Jamie again, and a draught of misery went through her, shutting away all else, even Nigel at her side.

She saw him glance at her. 'Perhaps I shouldn't——'

'No, no,' she said quickly: 'it's better to talk of things; I'd rather you did.' Whether this was true or not, she wanted him to believe it; perhaps she herself in time would come to believe it.

'There was a boy at school — his father died suddenly and he got called out of the chemistry class because there'd been a telegram. He didn't come back for a week and when he did no one knew what to say to him. A *boy* died, I remember, about two years ago; he drowned when one of those rubber boats —

21

dinghies — got carried out to sea. Gipps —' (Giles Ransome, the Headmaster, she remembered) — 'Gipps told us all at Assembly the first day of the autumn term——' His words came suddenly to a stop.

'I remember about that.' She wanted to assure him that nothing he said could distress her; it was the comfort of his presence that she needed.

'He wasn't a very nice boy, the one who got carried out to sea, but afterwards I used to think of things I'd said to him, and wish I hadn't.'

'Oh . . . yes, that always happens.'

They turned back towards the hotel. As they walked through the quiet of evening, with the hills nearly lost now, she thought that he was puzzling in his mind to form something that he hadn't said.

Maybe it would come out later: a sudden weariness, a formidable lack of energy prevented her from asking him more.

§

The day had a dark brilliance: she had dressed so often to go out with Jamie, for dinner with friends, for holidays, for climbing. Now she dressed for a time when he could not see her, and would not see her again. Her fingers shook and there was a nervous sickness within her, but the day was possible, as perhaps, she thought, all things are possible for a short time, even that last walk to the scaffold. The small graveyard of Borrowdale lay within the clasp of steep fellsides, the little barn-shaped church presented its frost-white walls and open door to the mountain air and the sound of cattle, as if these were part of its ceremony, and this no different from any other service.

Perfectly possible to endure this, with Nigel beside her in a dark suit which was a little too large for him, having been lent by Mark. She didn't scream or faint or even, she thought, behave very differently from her usual self. If she wept, it was not greatly noticeable, and did little, as weeping in full force sometimes can, to ease her.

Perhaps the Arctic strangeness of knowing that Jamie was no longer beside her set everything at a distance, like the first steps in a foreign country when the language and the streets, and even the cast of face is different from what one has known.

Now and again sunlight made brilliant the jewelled windows of

22

the church and washed the wet grass of the graveyard with a stream of gold. The bell in the small tower rang its summons and farewell; the single sound echoed down the valley, and cows from the neighbouring field came to the gate and looked on it all with mournful placid eyes, occasionally lowing as if in lament. . .

Now the company were all outside the church, and it was possible to see the coloured anoraks of walkers as they climbed a distant path, concerned only with the strenuous and welcome day. The many sheaves of flowers shivered in the wind like frail wings exposed too early to the cold. Soon it would be over, this extraordinary, malignant and final day. She herself shivered; Nigel beside her stood straight and serious, his hair ruffled. As they left the church he had taken her arm with a curious ease and maturity.

Almost done now. People trod warily, unsteady on the rough ground; all their faces looked as if they'd been painted with the same clay-coloured brush. The Vicar's cassock blew astream and his nose was red from cold. She tried to concentrate on the tremendous words he spoke; perhaps later they would return to her, but at the moment her mind was adrift: we are all standing, she thought, like people on a platform after the train has gone, heavy with the knowledge of departure, of the unknown. All parting, perhaps, was but a rehearsal: the farewells before a journey, that last sight of waving hands, even the departure of friends from one's home and the return to the empty room, the used glasses, the dented cushions and the new vibrating silence . . .

Now it was nearly done. She glanced about her, surprised to see faces that she knew: Sarah and David; people from the hotel; old climbing companions, some from far off — and, of course, Jamie's father.

What did he feel? Impossible to know: grief, she supposed, of a kind, for it was surely not possible for a widower to look on the death of his only son without pain. Yet he had always been a remote figure, an Anglican Minister, antipathetic to Jamie's climbing, antipathetic it seemed even to Jamie himself, certainly to her as Jamie's wife: long ago their meetings had dwindled, her small efforts at friendship had finally shrivelled, gone to nothing.

But now? She gave him a glance across this unwelcome place, where the stones were chill as the wind, but he was not looking her way; the lean face, thin grey hair adrift, was set in anonymous silence, nothing shown. Yet grief of a kind there must be: and she met a strange shaft of resentment, for it seemed that she wanted all the grief to herself, that to look on someone else who mourned Jamie as she did was not to find common ground, but an enemy. She had not the energy to be shocked by this; nothing at this time could be shocking, for everything was new, and all barriers down.

Over now. Hands and bodies chilled, faces held in respect, in sympathy, in sorrow, the company began to move, to let solemnity slip, like travellers who see harbour after a rough voyage. The company seemed larger than she had supposed, with a cameraman at a distance.

Nigel walked at her side. He looked as if he had been rowing strenuously on the river in the force of a March wind. She felt a shaft of love so acute that after this final farewell it seemed a savage thing, too much for her strength. This she must keep within herself; the sensation that she grasped at a sliding rope, almost swamped by a depth of cold sea.

Though chill light lay on the tops of the fells, the new upturned earth which she left behind lay in shadow. Nigel looked back. She reminded herself that he had come of his own choice, and that this had after all been a dignified ceremony in the small church which he had seen many times, a landmark at the end of a climb as the path led home.

Back at the hotel, a buffet had been laid in a small room looking out on the beck which slipped its seal-grey water outwards to the lake. This sound stayed in her head, accompanying an occasion which had the dimensions but not the blessed unreality of a dream. She spoke from some part of her head that was mercifully anaesthetized, yet able to function: she thought with surprise that one could do anything by making one's body move.

Even now, the moments were passing; her ear, tuned to the tireless running of the beck, nevertheless caught such words as 'get the train'; 'give you a lift'; already this time was changing, the company beginning to disband.

What would happen after this?

She glanced quickly about her, losing her detachment, aware of the people who were preparing to go. She had an impulse to keep them with her, to shut the doors, for instinct told her that the time after this would be different and was to be feared.

But of course, Nigel would be with her for a little while; Sarah and David too. And Jamie's father, the Reverend Clyde Rutherford. As if she had called to him, he came towards her.

You are still here, she thought; part of the known world, while

24

Jamie. . .

He said, 'At least, now we must be friends.'

'Of course.'

'Any help you need——'

'Oh — thank you. I'll be all right.'

'Spiritual help, perhaps; our faith surely teaches that those we love are only temporarily out of our sight.'

She said, 'Yes.' Possibly this was true: it did little to change the void at her heart. Nor did she at this time believe that she and Jamie's father would be better friends than they had been because of the loss of her husband and his son.

He said, 'If at any time you want to come and stay——'

She remembered the Norfolk vicarage with the draughts blowing through, the large rooms crowded with dark furniture; the long garden, once tended by Jamie's mother but now neglected and overgrown, with the swing splintered and sagging, held in what seemed to be a perpetual autumn afternoon.

He went on, 'The young man could come too — could you, Nigel?'

'Yes, Grandfather.'

She could not imagine that any more than herself did Nigel want to revisit the vicarage which would be more greatly shadowed, now that Jamie would never come there again. She could even now remember the boy's unease as he trailed through the large rooms, or stood yawning in the ancient church. (Yet the church, she remembered, had made a kindly imprint on her mind: a fifteenth-century wool church, tall with clear glass windows, and the pale shadows of stone.)

Jamie's father said, 'You could come any time; you would have only to let me know.'

About to make some neutral acknowledgement she saw that there were tears in his eyes, and before he turned away he put a hand on her shoulder.

I'm not sure of anything, she thought, for the gesture had moved her, and she saw Clyde suddenly not as an alien figure, but a man who perceived perhaps in her and Nigel all that endured for him in the day-to-day world.

No, nothing is certain, she thought; and knew a touch of sudden deep fear, as if the loss of Jamie were in some way to be lived over again.

Nonsense, of course; a legacy of this day which was now ending. When the company was gone, she said to Nigel, 'Is there anything you'd like to do?'

'I thought I might go for a walk. If you don't mind.'

'No, of course not.' Clear that he wanted to go alone — better so, perhaps; for a little while he should be free of this. She watched him go; he had taken off his formal jacket and wore a large red sweater. The colour glowed, like new life.

Slowly, evening flooded the valley. Nigel had not returned. He could not surely have gone far, but the stress of this unaccountable day had left her too readily apprehensive, and she found herself watching for him as she had watched for the return of the climbing party, and seen Sarah coming towards the hotel in the rain.

When he at last returned, her relief was out of all proportion. This she withheld, saying only as he pulled off his sweater, 'Where did you go?'

'Just round about.' His skin was coloured by the evening wind. 'I went a little way up the Watendlath path.' She could see the fellside path, from which the valley with its tall heads was spread before you in calm symmetry. She said, 'You can see the church from there.'

'Yes.' He was absently pulling the sleeves of his sweater the right way out. 'I went down to the churchyard afterwards. I went to look at the grave.' He spoke quite naturally; she drew her hands over her face. He went on, 'It was filled in: the flowers were there, but there wasn't anybody about. It seemed better to see it like that. You can't think with people around.'

Certainly that had been true, but she could not have returned to the grave, alone, in the evening light.

His eyes were on her. 'Was it a bad thing to do?'

'Why no — of course not.'

'I understand things better when I have them to myself.'

Yes; this confused, momentous afternoon had not been entirely real: she had recognised grief like a figure seen through a crowd; she had not been alone with the quiet and terrible grave.

As if perhaps he took her thought he said, 'I shouldn't go there if I were you. You look pretty done in.'

'No,' she said, grateful; 'I won't go.'

Guests were coming down the stairs; she heard a man say, 'Time for a drink before dinner? Yes, I think so.'

A drink before dinner. Even this day would come to an end, she

26

thought, with the mountain heads drowned in the dark. And the new time would begin.

2

She turned in the silent London room. This was the new time, some weeks old. Claudia's pie was still on the table. She sat as one sits when waiting for the doorbell to ring. She did not know how long she sat there. She hoped it was a long time, but when she looked at her watch only a quarter of an hour had passed: it was two o'clock.

Curious, this feeling of impermanence, like being in a waiting-room on a journey, with time suspended. She would fill in this hour or the next: write a letter or go for a walk, but purpose seemed fundamentally absent. Curious, too, this sensation of danger, for of course all that was past: the danger of the rocks, of the climb, of the fall. . . There could be nothing dangerous in this quiet room.

Unless. . . She rose to her feet (a restlessness afflicted her, whose other side was lethargy). What had someone written, in one of the many letters of condolence? . . . 'It's such a cold country one lives in alone.'

Perhaps too cold? 'That which I greatly feared has come upon me.' She couldn't remember who'd said that, but it was true, and for long spaces of time it didn't seem possible to live alone, to live without Jamie, to live without love. Sharp and savage memories, combined with the smallest physical reminders (his sticks in the hall; his writing upon a page) produced a sensation, an actual pain like a clenched hand in her chest, as though someone had tied a knot in her lungs. Rather like the prelude to vomiting, and like sickness it erupted every now and again in a bout of weeping, noisy, pointless, hard to restrain: mercifully, when she was alone.

But if this toothache of the spirit could not be endured, what then?

She walked through the flat, as she had walked so often before in these last weeks, as if looking for something, but of course there was nothing to find. There was this place which was empty, and slow time going past, to be endured somehow; no palliative but the cry to a God who seemed so far away for help.

She thought, I don't know about God. When things were all right, I thought he was there, a benign mist, someone to whom one said Thank you, or asked for balm in trouble. Now . . . it's like someone who promises to hold you in the water, and then suddenly when you think you're drowning, there's no one there. Only silence, the same silence that comes when the front door shuts behind me after I've been out: the silence which is the worst thing.

But danger?

She stood still, trying to think it out. She had been afraid of the new time; she had been unprepared for the force of its desolation. Words had come her way, of help, of advice, of warning. They said that when the person who had been part of each minute of every day for more than twenty years died, some part of you died too, and what was left was jumbled and fragmented, like a bombed house, its purpose gone. Perhaps she was a little mad; one couldn't know. One couldn't even, she thought, explain, for it was not like being sad or anxious or even distraught (though it was at times all of these): it was a condition, partly physical, which took light and colour and meaning from everything she said and did.

So after that? A way out?

She stood with the silence about her, the pie on the table, the sounds, unheard, drifting up from the street. The well-meaning voices again returned to her: ring up your friends (but what does one say? — for it was not always possible to speak of desolation; one had been taught somewhere along the line not to do it); come and *see* us; get out of the flat; realise that life must go on, that you are part of it; come out, come and see, you must be brave. . . If not brave, she had been obedient, gone to stay with friends, visited an old lady house-bound by arthritis, typed a woman friend's history of the Peninsular War. Briefly she would become absorbed, then the dread would return. No more than anything else could she explain the dread, the twist of fear at the pit of her stomach. (Though there were others who knew about it: a woman after a luncheon party — all widows — who had run after her in the sunlight of the drive to say, 'Believe me, the anguish *does* pass.')

But if it did not?

She turned again in the room. There seemed, within this darkness, to be an investigator, as if she stood in the dock.

'What d'you mean, Mrs Rutherford, by "danger"?'

'I don't know.'

'You spoke of a way out——'

'Yes, well, I've thought about that.'

'I think you must make yourself plain. You mean that you'd be prepared to do away with yourself?'

'It'd be a solution——'

'Cowardly, you'll agree?'

'Oh yes, I expect so.'

'Selfish too.'

'Yes. But one can get beyond all that; one can lose heart.'

'Let me put a proposition to you, Mrs Rutherford. Suppose your doctor came to you and said "I can give you a jab with this needle and you won't know anything about it, and it will all seem perfectly natural; there won't be any stigma of suicide; I shan't get into any trouble, and your family won't have any more difficulty than is normally attendant on death" — would you say "Yes, go ahead?"'

'No ... no, I wouldn't.'

'Are you sure of that?'

'Yes; there's Nigel, after all.'

'Precisely: your son. A gift from God.' (The investigator seemed to have taken Holy Orders.)

'There was a song I once heard, sentimental, Victorian: "I loved you in life too little; I loved you in death too much." There's the rub; the times I failed in love, and I failed often.'

'We all fail, Mrs Rutherford. In every human endeavour, more or less. And there are other failures, and other pains——'

'I know, I know. Grief is selfish; I know that.'

'But you can go on, putting one foot in front of the other, enduring each five minutes as it comes?'

'Yes, I suppose I can do that.'

'Then that's all that's asked of you. For the present.'

'I'm not doing very well, am I?'

'I've known those who did worse. It's no good, you know, being afraid of the future. We're all, one way or another, afraid of that and we all get to the end somehow. One is afraid of death just as one is afraid of life.'

'My own death seems different now. I think sometimes, there is this great change to come, and "slow how e'er my marches be, I shall at length sit down by thee."'

'And you believe that?'

'I don't know ... I'm sure of nothing — only of a fragmentary hope. I can't believe I shall see and hear Jamie again — *hear* above all, because a voice *is* a person — not as he was, and how can I imagine anything else — a shape, an essence? I can't talk to that, hold that, love that...'

'You have to trust.'

'I'll try.'

'You have to learn to be a whole person, living alone. Living without your husband.'

'I haven't yet.'

'May I suggest, Mrs Rutherford, that you write some of your feelings down? The mere effort of writing will put them at a distance.'

'Very well.'

The voice appeared to cease. Obedient, she took pages of foolscap and pen. It would be something to do, it would occupy the fathomless time... For whom did she write? For no one; perhaps for Nigel, one day... She wrote across the head of the paper 'Perhaps for Nigel', and began.

She wrote for some time, until her wrist ached and ink stained her fingers. When she had no more to say, she left the pages on her desk, not concerned with them any more.

It was true that the effort had put pain at a small distance. Absently she picked up the morning's letters again, glanced at them, then put them down. She wondered for how long letters would come addressed to Jamie. Perhaps for ever, since there would always be someone in New Zealand who wouldn't know, some editor of a reference book on Men of Moment who would send out questionnaires... Not one of the worst things; merely the small errors of official life.

What now? She turned, as if for an answer, to the photograph of Nigel on the mantelpiece. Half-term was close now; it would be so good to see him again. Only a long week-end, but you could do much in a week-end, especially in early summer — perhaps a day on the river for he loved the river and ships. As she looked at the photograph she recalled their walk together in Borrowdale and the sensation that he had a question, left unsaid... Perhaps he would tell her, when he came.

But until then?

She rose with an abrupt movement, as if in decision, though she had made none. She went to the cupboard and pulled out the pile of frayed notebooks. She hadn't before opened the cupboard; this was a new thing. Done without thought, not without fear. She knelt on the floor, on the sun-warmed carpet. The notebooks surrounded her; she'd forgotten there were so many of them.

She opened the first that came to hand. Dated more than ten years ago, the paper staled, the ink clear but old. Jamie's handwriting, with its decorative energy: all right, she thought, I can read it; I've got to read it some time...

She read: 'Clogwyn du'r Arddu — East Buttress. April, cold, still patches of snow. Some difficulty on the third pitch...'

Yes, perfectly possible to read: she was even drawn into the stories of these climbs, which, though she hadn't taken part in, she could remember.

She read from another book; her hand steady as she turned the page; only a sense of threat made her read greedily, with passion.

'Pico de Aneto in the Maladeta Massif — the Cursed Mountains — how well the Spaniards name their terrible hills! The day began badly with heavy storm, such as only the Pyrenees can produce with quite such suddenness; but one's known bad weather before, and the day has gone well. The sun never showed itself...' She read on, more swiftly; she read of the accident to one of the climbing party, Gerald Furness, who broke a leg in a fall... 'It was a streaming, benighted day: the Spanish rescue team brought to our disaster all their mingled pity and relish for violent mischance... Only one blessed thing: when we got back to the Cabane where we were staying, Eve was there, and she healed all wounds as she always does — we can fight sometimes, but when things go badly she gives everything you need: never puts a foot wrong...'

At first she sat crouched on the floor, only aware that she had stopped reading. The note-books were spread about her on the carpet. Then the knot in her chest became jagged, like the clutch of cramp, and she wept with tears that seemed to come from some deep of misery, as yet unvisited. Nothing would stop them, for Jamie was clear before her, in the Rosthwaite hotel, prepared for his last climb, and he was saying, 'I'm never glad you're not there'; and it was almost the last thing he had said to her, and it was true, and she had paid it so little attention: now it seemed that this small failure, which couldn't be repaired, was the cause of all her grief.

She kept saying, 'Please come back; please come back.' She felt ugly and messy and useless with tears. 'Oh, please come back.' But the impossibility of what she asked met her like the slam of a door, and the weeping continued to tear through her like the rigor of a disease. 'I have to stop,' she said to herself; 'I have to stop; this is just a tiresome thing, a kind of self-pity. I have to stop.' But that slam of the final door: the juxtaposition of his image in her mind with the knowledge that search where she would, across the world or in the skies, she could not find him again nor hear his voice kept the weeping in force, until with the suddenness of a slap from the outside world, the doorbell rang.

This brought her to silence with a gasp, as if she came up from cold water. She scrambled to her feet and scrubbed her face with a handkerchief. The bell rang again, and compulsion took hold: this was a time with panic woven within it; any summons — door or telephone — roused sudden fear. She made one more attempt to wipe her face, then opened the door.

At first she shook her head, as if to clear it from imagination.

But it was true. Nigel stood there, suitcase beside him (fastened by one lock, the other open and a tie escaping from the case). He looked as he always did on arrival, as if he were haunted by some perhaps bewildering event on the journey.

'*Nigel!*'

'Hullo, Ma.' She saw at once that he had taken in her scrubbed face, her disordered hair. The last thing she wanted.

'But I didn't expect you till — oh, never mind that: I'm so glad to see you!' This was so much more true than she could express that she smiled at it.

She hugged him briefly, and he put his suitcase down in the middle of the floor. 'I wrote you a letter.'

'Oh — posts! I haven't had it.' (Had she ever chided him for such things as a half-locked suitcase, and a tendency to put everything — coat or case or scarf — in the middle of the room?) 'I really am so *glad* to see you,' she said again, for an hilarious relief was running through her which could only find expression in the most banal and repetitive phrases. She saw his glance go over the scattered notebooks on the floor, and she began hurriedly to put them together.

Nigel picked up two of them, then sat on a chair. She sat too, with the books clasped on her lap. He said, 'I don't expect that was a good thing to do——'

'No, it wasn't. I had a sort of impulse: there seemed so much time, and nothing to do with it.' She smiled at him, not knowing whether he understood.

His head was bent over one of the notebooks, which he had opened. 'I wouldn't look at them for a bit,' he said, closing the book.

'No, I shan't.'

'Poor Ma; I'm sorry. I expect it's all been fairly foul.' He looked round the room as if he saw it in new perspective. 'This place . . . it's a bit full of him, isn't it? Is it a good idea for you to stay here?'

'Yes —' she made further efforts to smooth her hair — 'Yes, I think so. I think so. As long as I can. You can't be very sure of anything, not at first. But when I go away, I want to get back. I don't mean I think he's going to be here, or anything daft like that. But it seems to be home.'

He nodded. 'I expect it's more difficult now.'

She was more and more surprised at his quiet and adult perception. Possible that his father's death had brought him to sudden maturity?

'Oh yes,' she said; 'yes, it is. People try to do things from time to time, but of course. . .'

His glance went to the pie on the table. 'Is that your lunch?'

'Not exactly. Claudia from downstairs brought it for me, but . . . I wasn't hungry.'

'I expect you ought to eat it.' His young face looked doubtful. 'But if you're not going to, d'you mind if I have it? Breakfast seems ages ago.'

'Of course! Here——' She hurried to get knife and fork; it seemed a small but joyful thing that he should eat the pie, and that she could lay a place for him.

He gave her a smile, as if in apology, and ate with enthusiasm and speed. When he'd finished, he said, 'That was gorgeous; I really was terribly hungry.' Wiping his mouth he took both plate and suitcase out of the room; hurriedly she combed her hair and repaired her face. When he returned, he sat in doubtful silence, as if in indecision.

To help him, she said, 'What did you say in your letter?'

'I — I just told you I'd be coming *this* Saturday, not next. I got the date wrong, you see. And. . .'

She waited.

'Well — I've got a week; not just the week-end——'

'Why, that's lovely!'

'Yes, but I thought, I thought that I'd stay here until — until Wednesday, and then go for a few days to Mark.'

She had time in the brief seconds before she spoke to control the fall of disappointment. 'Why, of course. If you want to.'

He seemed relieved, yet not quite sure of himself. More to come? She must not, must not say that his presence here was life, and that she was afraid of the closing of the door when he went, with his suitcase packed, to Mark Stevens and then on to school.

He still looked puzzled. In what way had she failed? Perhaps not at all, or perhaps the failure lay deep in herself, perhaps she needed too much. She said quickly, 'I've never seen their house; have you a photograph?'

He shook his head. 'It's just a sort of house with a garden; there's an apple tree and a lawn. And of course the pool.'

She saw goldfish. 'Pretty.'

'No, I mean a swimming-pool.'

'Honestly? It sounds ... grand.'

'Not really. The pool isn't awfully big, but you can swim, and sit beside it in the summer ... I don't really know why we're talking about the swimming-pool.'

'I asked you about the house. Are they very well off, Mark's parents?'

'I don't know what very well off is any more. They seem to have all the things they want, or most of them. Two cars and the house and lots of drinks. But they don't *look* rich — at least Mark's father doesn't — he wears quite shabby clothes when he's off duty. Mark says he's a bit thick, but I'm not sure. I rather like him. Mrs Stevens wears lots of make-up and tight slacks. I think she *is* rather silly, and I think Mark agrees, but he never says so. She isn't intelligent like you.'

The small compliment surprised her. After a moment or two he said, 'You remember about this summer, don't you?'

'This summer?'

'Daddy must've talked to you about it.'

'I don't know ... talked about what?'

'This Spanish lark. Daddy came up and signed the permission form. It was half-term; I think you had flu.'

Dimly she could remember the half-term, and the attack of flu. Yes, Jamie had gone north to the school in Derbyshire — she could remember little else except that she had missed Jamie, and her happiness at his return. 'Permission?' she said.

'You have to have a parent's permission,' he said.

She felt stupid, as if her recent outbreak of grief had muddled her wits. He went on, 'It's not till September. Just before term starts.'

'September?'

'About a dozen of us are going. It's all settled. They have to arrange these things in January, months and months ahead. Dad must've told you about it.'

Had he? She tried to think. 'I don't know.'

'He was keen on the idea — at least, when we were talking about it. After that he didn't say much more——'

Yes, she could remember *that* of Jamie: his sudden enthusiasms, the rapidity with which he would move on to the next thing, impatient, full of prospects, plans and ideas.

'I don't remember anything about it. He may have told me but I can't remember.' Glancing at him, she thought that this had been on his mind for some time.

He said, 'It's perfectly all right — safe, I mean.'

'Safe?'

'Larry Howard's coming with us; he's done this sort of thing heaps of times before: you know how he is about sports, ice-cold water and fresh air——'

Larry Howard was Nigel's Housemaster. 'Yes, I remember that.'

'Even Dad said he was a good reliable climber.'

'Climber?'

'Nothing like Dad, of course, but terribly reliable. I know you always found him a bit hearty — well, he is, but very *careful*.'

She didn't repeat the word, because she seemed to be repeating every word he said.

He went on, 'There's another master coming with us: Gene Carson. You'd like him: he's quite young, and one of those Canadians who make you feel everything's easy. We hire a couple of jeeps in the town, and then go up into the mountains and camp there and climb a bit.'

'Mountains——'

'The Pyrenees. We stay in Andorra — it's between France and Spain.'

'Jamie climbed in the Pyrenees.' Her glance went to the notebooks, piled on the table. 'It was there that they had the accident, when Gerald Furness——'

'I know. I remember Dad talking about that. But this isn't the same part: that was in the Maladeta; Andorra's more to the right,

36

I mean east; it's a place where tourists go now; you can get there from Perpignan or Barcelona——'

'I know where it is. Jamie and I came home that way once, driving from Spain. There's a long road — it goes on and on and up and up ... must have been about ten years ago, perhaps more.' The endless, spiralling journey returned to her, and with it some twist of apprehension. 'The mountains are very steep — they close in, not like the Lakes or Wales, not like that at all.'

'We're camping near a village,' he said; 'it's a proper site; Boy Scouts and people like that go there.'

She could see only the long climbing road, the steep mountains, the small tongue of land between river and mountain foot. The river ran fast, she remembered, oyster grey and green: had not she been told of a child drowned there, the body carried at a great pace away?

'So you planned to go there... No, I don't remember anything about it.'

'Dad signed the form.'

'Yes — yes, I'm sure he did.' Jamie, though pleased by the idea, would not have taken much account of it; he'd said nothing to her, perhaps forgotten, intending to speak later... She was surprised to feel a sudden urge of anger: all very well to sign his name like that, give the all-clear, but now——

Anger. Strange to feel anger when only a short while ago she had been weeping in the desolation of lost love. But of course anger had been sometimes part of life; perhaps it was part of death too.

She said, 'I'm trying to get this straight. You're going on an expedition in the summer——'

'Early September. Before the autumn term.'

'Isn't that rather late in the season?'

'I honestly don't know: I shouldn't think so. I believe package tours go on until the end of September. Then they start ski-ing.'

'Is Mark going with you?'

She noticed the colour that came on his face. 'Yes, he is.'

'I didn't think Mark was the outdoor kind.'

'Well, I suppose he isn't as a rule. But this is abroad, and Mark likes abroad. He likes anything he can talk about afterwards that sounds good.'

This unexpected detachment (for he came always strongly to Mark's defence) was, she recognised, inherited from his father, who was accurate, if merciful, in his judgements. Unlike herself who was too anxious to please.

'So Mark's going,' she said, 'yes, I see.'

'It'll be more fun to have him there. After all, he is my friend.'

Mark came again to her mind: hands in his pockets, the downward, half-scornful smile. A figure of ill-omen, she thought, but the words were of course too absurd to be spoken.

She said at last, 'No, I didn't know anything about the trip. I'm sure I didn't.'

§

It was on the evening before his going to Mark's, after dinner, that she spoke.

'Super meal,' he said, wiping his mouth. 'Thanks. Wine too.'

'Just because it's your last night.'

'Well — for now. I'll be back.'

'Of course. Yes, of course.' She swallowed, for the moment to speak was here. No time to consider whether or not it was wise: that other person who had been Jamie's wife would have had control, reason and sanity: that person was gone. She said, 'I don't want you to go to Andorra.'

'Don't *want* me to?'

'No. Not yet. Not so soon.'

'It isn't till September.'

'No, but — if you could postpone it.'

'How could I? It's all arranged.'

'There'd be another chance — next year.'

'Next year I'll be starting A levels. Everyone goes now, when the summer exams are over.'

'Everyone?'

'Well — the ones who want to. And in any case — a *year*. That's ages: anything could happen in a year. It won't be the same.'

'You mean Mark might not be going?'

His eyes were away from her, his mouth set in disappointment. 'I suppose he mightn't. I don't know — how can anyone know about a year ahead?'

You had to remember what length of time a year must seem to him. A year was an eternity in youth, whereas for her it was nothing. Only the word 'year' carried some overtone of the past, of a long road.

She said, 'If it were somewhere else——'

'What's wrong with Andorra?'

'I don't know. I don't know.' She could see the long climbing road in the narrow defile between the mountains. Had not the weather changed, so that the fir-crowded depths, thousands of feet below, turned dark and fathomless? 'It was a lonely place, I remember: nothing but a few grey cottages and farms and peasants: it might have belonged to another age.'

He said that it was quite different now; and repeated that Boy Scouts went there, as if this were the ultimate in security. 'It's just a sort of outdoor exercise: nothing could go wrong.'

'You say Jamie gave permission——'

'Yes.'

'Then you have to *have* permission?'

'Yes — "parent or guardian". You know how schools have to cover themselves, in case some drippy parent comes along and says their little boy's got chilblains or athlete's foot.'

'And when you say Jamie agreed, you mean that's settled it?'

He looked at her, looked away. 'I suppose now . . . they'd want your permission too.'

She was silent. It was there. She had this small power. His eyes were on her with pleading, but she could see only Jamie's face, quiet in death.

As she didn't speak, he went on, 'You wouldn't want to stop me — would you?'

'Would it mean so much?'

He looked puzzled, perhaps defeated. 'Yes — I suppose it would. I've got these filthy exams, and it'd be something to look forward to.'

Unanswerable: that other self, who had walked in sanity, would have been eager to give in to him.

'You could do something else. Mark too.'

'But it's all *fixed*——' He broke off. 'I'm sorry. I suppose I can see why you don't want me to go. But — honestly — there isn't any danger.'

She was again silent, seeing the high mountains, formidable and close; the cut of an eagle's wing against the sky. Far places, full of menace.

She looked at him across the table, the remains of his meal now abandoned: these spoke of failure. She didn't want failure now, when tomorrow he would be gone.

She said, 'It's not till September. Don't let's talk about it any more.'

'All right.' He looked relieved, a burden set down. 'You don't mind me going to Mark's tomorrow?'

'No, no, of course not.' It wasn't true, but perhaps he didn't know that. And the future threat could wait.

§

Some time in the small hours, Nigel woke. At first he was unable to locate the sensation of unease in his mind; then he remembered the discussion about Andorra and his mother's resistance. She had said no more; they had talked easily enough of other things.

But at this unaccustomed hour, when the house gave only the plaint of water-pipes and the joint-crack of furniture, as if in relief after the day, the question wouldn't go from his mind. At last he climbed out of bed and went barefoot in his pyjamas to the kitchen. Here he made himself a glass of lemonade and found a packet of biscuits. As he carried these past the living-room, the glow from a table-lamp caught his eye.

He paused, held in curiosity, even apprehension. Burglars? Surely not. And his mother's bedroom door had been shut, her room dark.

He looked into the living-room. No sign of a burglar, or indeed of anyone. The clock on the mantelpiece pointed half-past two. Barefoot, he crept towards the light which was beside the writing desk. On the desk itself lay some pages of foolscap paper, covered with his mother's handwriting. She must have gone to bed (some while after him) and left the light on. Sometimes, he remembered, she had left lights on and his father had shown mild exasperation.

He made to turn off the switch, when words at the top of the page arrested him.

Perhaps for Nigel?

Nothing, he thought, like one's own name to command attention, even allow one to read, though he'd been taught not to read other people's letters, and couldn't remember that he'd ever done so.

But this wasn't a letter: it was (perhaps) for him. And the first words transfixed him: 'We talk to each other, we say acceptable things; then we go home and throw ourselves out of the window.'

He sat abruptly in the chair, as if moved by shock. The light lay like a finger which pointed to the written pages. He read on, able to do nothing else. He read of the transitory sense of waiting, the silence, the unaccountable fear. (The fear which had driven her to oppose his holiday?) He read, 'Before, there was a bridge that one followed, knowing that in spite of all problems, the bridge would still be there each day; now each time I wake it seems as if I had to take a new block to stand on: build the bridge as I go along. Beyond that, there's nothing, only the dark. . .'

The room had a chill which he'd not noticed before; his feet were cold. He read on, through this hastily written chronicle of grief. 'Perhaps it's been of some help to write this; it's not important, only the sketch map of a personal journey . . . perhaps not even for Nigel to read.'

The writing ended. The room was silent, the lamp still burned. Now he knew he should not have read the pages; perhaps he had known from the beginning.

Not before, he thought, had he learned so much of another person, as if he had listened at a door. He switched off the lamp, took his biscuits and lemonade to bed. But the words stayed with him, and he lay long awake.

3

When Nigel got down from the train the small station brought a scent of early summer, open skies, different from the town. He walked quickly, carrying his case along the quiet road. The road left the village behind and climbed gently past the few houses whose gardens showed amongst their abundance early roses and primulas, but no sign of other life.

The Stevens' house stood away from the road, at the end of a lane which climbed between hedgerows. As before, this path held magic, for he would see Mark at the end of it. Now more than ever he wanted his company: they would wander off alone, and it would be all right when he had talked with Mark whose presence would solve all anxieties. Nigel looked forward to this with the whole-hearted passion of youth in trouble.

The prospect of the house faced him, as apparently lifeless as all the other houses. But on so fine a day, the Stevens would most likely be in the garden. Perhaps he would find Mark alone: he hoped so.

He made straight for the garden by the path which led between house and garage, then stopped. The pool, the swing seat, the deck-chairs, were all empty; the garage had been empty too. Perhaps the adults had gone out, and Mark was somewhere in the house.

He put down his case and wiped his forehead. He didn't like the signs of many people's presence: glasses, cups and saucers, ashtrays, a man's jacket thrown over one of the garden chairs. He called 'Mark?' but there was no answer. The french window from the living-room stood ajar; he pushed it and went in.

The room was dim after the sunlight. At first he thought the room was empty. He was about to turn away when movement caught his eye.

Sudden movement, but not so sudden that he had not seen two figures, a man and a woman, clasped together in the armchair. His first sensation was one of disagreeable shock, for though he had seen couples lying together on summer grass, in London

42

parks or in the country, he had never seen anyone he knew. And this woman at least he knew, for it was Mark's mother.

She stood, flushed, hair awry, her summer dress crumpled. Anger followed the surprise on her face. 'Nigel! What are you doing, walking in here——' She stopped; he saw the brief struggle to regain dignity. The man, a stranger to him, stood with a look of blank reserve. He was broad and dark, perhaps fifty, with grey in plentiful black hair: coarsely handsome, a mixture of the pirate and the businessman.

Mark's mother had put anger away; her pretty face with its large eyes and small nose wore now a bright, perhaps pleading smile.

'We didn't expect you till later; Mark said late afternoon.'

'I caught an earlier train.'

'This is Henry, Henry Boyle. Nigel Rutherford, Mark's great friend.'

Henry Boyle leaned with one arm on the mantelpiece. 'Hullo, young man. Don't think we've met.' He was almost recovered; not quite, Nigel thought.

'Henry came down for the day with his son Lynton; they've all gone off for a drive——'

'Mark as well?'

'Yes.'

Embarrassment rested now, he thought, only with himself; Henry Boyle had lit a cigarette and strolled across the room; Mrs Stevens was as he remembered her; it was almost as if he had dreamed that scuffle in the chair.

'When will they be back?'

'Oh — quite soon. Meanwhile I expect you'd like to go to your room. . .'

He was glad to leave them. Once in his bedroom, he looked from the window to the garden and the swimming-pool. The unwelcome discovery downstairs still haunted him. Henry Boyle and his son Lynton. . . He'd heard Mark speak of Lynton Boyle who, so far as he recalled, was two years older and had just gone up to Cambridge . . . had not his name, as Nigel saw it, occurred too frequently in conversation?

He pulled the clothes out of his suitcase with an anger born of disappointment. Mark wasn't here, when he so greatly needed him. On the way here he had imagined his arrival: Mark's parents perhaps off for the day: Mark himself waiting for him, even on the look-out. It had not been like that at all. He flung socks and under-pants into a drawer. Though he heard the sounds of arrival down-stairs, he made no effort to leave his room. At last Mark came to find him.

'Hi,' Mark said.

Nigel didn't turn, taking a sock from the drawer as if it inter-ested him. In the looking-glass he could see Mark standing there, leaning against the jamb of the door. Dark hair fell over his fore-head, one eyebrow slightly lifted. He was of course clear what was wrong. 'Sorry I wasn't here, but the Boyles came down without warning, and you know what that's like: everything goes haywire.'

'Suppose so. Where's Lynton?'

'Having a drink downstairs.'

Nigel shut the drawer. 'Is he staying to dinner?'

The image in the looking-glass didn't change. 'Don't think so. Lynton's mother's expecting them back. And from what I under-stand all hell can get loose if she's made some sort of mess with asparagus and they don't turn up. Or so Lynton says.'

Nigel glanced up at Lynton's name, but said only, 'I wanted to talk to you.'

'Well, so you can, when they've gone . . . Coming downstairs?'

'In a moment.'

Alone, Nigel stared down at the garden where the shadow had begun to divide it, but saw more clearly the sunlight on the empty spaces of his mother's flat, and the lamplit pages of her chronicle which he had guiltily read. While he had been there pity and dis-comfort had made him wish to escape; but now with this uncom-fortable arrival, he half-wished to be back.

Nothing was simple, he reflected, as he went once more into the living-room. Voices were loud and full of laughter: Mark's mother was talking with composure and amusement to Henry Boyle. Observing them, Nigel was puzzled by the falsity of social communication, for they were talking like easy friends, and it was almost impossible to recall that scuffle in the chair. If this could be so easily and quickly smothered, what other secrets lay beneath the benign chatter and decorous behaviour of people in company? Then he blushed, for he remembered his own secret, which he would have told to no one.

Mark's father, Rufus Stevens, greeted him with an ease which managed to contain compassion. While he made suitable replies, Nigel puzzled over the quality in Rufus Stevens which seemed at once to contain vulgarity and a lively perception.

Mark was talking to Lynton Boyle. Lynton had a swathe of bronze hair, a lean face with an aquiline nose, a mouth that laughed easily and a boneless way of movement. He was dressed in a dark blue short-sleeved shirt and cream-coloured slacks. He did not look at all like his father. He was talking about the cricket season.

'. . . but the West Indies, God, yes I know we've got to like them, and put up with all that carry on with tribal drums, but personally I like my game in its natural tomb-like quiet with only an occasional irruption from the plebs when they've drunk too well at the tavern and someone hits a boundary or a pigeon. . .'

Mark was laughing, his face different from the face which Nigel had seen just now in the looking-glass. He felt again nostalgia for the London room. He belonged there, was wanted there. Here the talk flowed over and past him. He stood silent, impatient for Mark to belong to him again, impatient to put his question.

The company at last wandered into the hall. Here they all stood, as if to step beyond the front door was forbidden. People can talk for *ever*, Nigel thought, and an image of his father came strongly to him: Jamie Rutherford, who liked to talk at ease with his wife or his friends, but found the endless barter of small exchanges on the doorstep a trial to his spirit. Nigel could remember his father's sigh and flop of relief into a chair when the visitors had gone: 'It's perfectly possible to say "Thank you" and walk through a front door: you'd think some sort of death-ray prevented them.'

When the Boyles had gone, Rufus Stevens came in from the garden, a jacket over his arm. 'Lynton left this behind.'

'Sign that he wants to come back,' Mark said, 'or so the Freudians tell us.'

Laura Stevens had the secret gaiety of a pretty woman lately admired. She took a glass from the mantelpiece, saying to her husband, 'Darling, I do wish you wouldn't put things up here; they leave a mark.'

'It'll wipe off.'

'We've only *just* had the place decorated——'

'I know; the bill came yesterday.'

Laura said, 'Mark, go and get a damp cloth from the kitchen.'

As she rubbed with perhaps unnecessary force at the surface of the mantelpiece, Rufus said, 'I daresay you two boys'd like a walk before dinner.'

At last; what Nigel had been hoping for all along. But not quite as he had hoped for it. As they went together through the gate at the end of the garden, and on to the shoulder of the tilted field, Mark said easily, 'Bit of a row blowing up.'

'Yes, I suppose there was.'

'Not worth it really. Ma likes the gentlemen to flatter her — she always has.'

The encounter in the drawing-room returned to Nigel's mind, but embarrassment prevented him from speaking of it. In any case he wasn't at the moment concerned with Mark's parents, or whatever dalliance Laura Stevens had a mind to. He said, 'Does Lynton often come here?'

Mark shrugged. 'Now and then.'

'D'you like him?'

'He's amusing.'

'Is that all a person has to be?'

'Well, of course not. But he is.'

'He's a lot older than you.'

'Two years ... so what?'

They had reached the top of the hill. The house below them lay now in shadow, but distant fields showed the yellow flags of char-lock made more brilliant by evening light. They sat together on the rough grass; warmth covered them like a light fleece, and the saw-drone of flies spoke of summer.

' "So" nothing,' Nigel said, pulling at a piece of grass. 'I wanted to talk to you.'

'Well, what cooks?'

His mother, Nigel said, didn't want him to go on the Andorran trip.

'Whyever not?'

'I suppose — I suppose, because of Father. I'm the only child——'

'Good God, you're not a pilot in the Battle of Britain; we're going on a package deal and the worst that'll happen to us is diarrhoea because of some disgusting foreign food.'

'I know. I know. I tried to explain that, but — well — she's got a thing about it. I suppose it isn't rational——'

'Mean she's nuts?'

'No. No. But Father's death was terribly sudden. He was forty-seven. I know that's quite old but it's not an age when people *die*

46

— not normally die. And when I first went up to Borrowdale she looked as if she'd been hit by a truck.'

Mark shifted his position on the grass. 'Well, I know it was ghastly, and we were all frightfully sorry——'

'That isn't what I mean. I don't want you to be sorry.'

'You're not trying to say you want to call it off?'

'No... no... just that I wanted to talk. About how she was. I came away feeling guilty about her.'

'Oh, God — *guilt*. Tiresome and absolutely no use to anyone. I've told you that before. Sort of self-indulgence.'

'Well, maybe, but I felt it. One of Father's climbing friends had an accident in the Pyrenees, some years ago... She just doesn't want me to go.'

Mark frowned, plucking at the grass. 'Tell her your father would have wanted you to.'

'I don't know if that's true.'

'I expect it is.'

'She's terribly cut up.'

'Sure — yes, of course she is. But it's — what — nearly two months ago.'

'I don't think that's awfully long.'

'By September it'll be longer.'

'I know, but——'

Mark turned his head. 'Don't you want to come?'

'Oh Lord — you *know* I do. It was one of the best things, when you said we'd sign on. But now——'

'It isn't any good, letting parents get on top of you. Yes; I know this is a bit extreme: your father and everything. But you have to take a stand, otherwise you get swamped.'

Nigel nodded, without conviction. The words of the chronicle persisted in his head, but he wouldn't speak of them. They at least were private. He said, 'You have to have a parent's permission. And Mother could refuse.'

'Oh Lord — she wouldn't do that. She couldn't — she's not that kind of person, what I've seen of her.'

'I don't think I know what kind of person she is now. I don't think perhaps she knows herself.'

'You've just got to stick it out.'

Nigel pulled a piece of grass in two. 'I didn't think it'd be so difficult.'

'It won't; you'll see.'

'When I got there — to the flat, I mean — she'd been crying. She looked awful.' For a moment he saw again Laura Stevens, pretty, admired, with a husband and, perhaps, a lover.

Mark's eyes were narrowed as he looked into the low evening sun. 'Well, I guess she did. But it won't go on like that.' He'd changed, Nigel thought; some trace of mockery had gone.

'How d'you know?'

'There's a friend of my mother's whose husband was killed in a car smash. I must say, she did look terrible at first — kind of puffy and white — but she's quite different now.'

'Oh, good. Only — how can you know? People look all right, but they aren't always, inside.'

Mark shrugged. 'Well, maybe not, but she seemed O.K. You wait. By September, it'll be fine. After all, they were always going off together, weren't they? Your parents?'

'They can't any more.'

'No, but — they *did* go. Off on their own, a lot of the time. Now it's your turn.'

Nigel lifted one hand to shade his eyes from the sun. Warmth and the scents of early summer blended with Mark's words to form comfort. Gradually the image of the London room and the lighted pages on the desk began to fade. He put his hand over the grass and touched Mark's as it lay there. It was easy to do that here, alone in the warm grass, with the house below lost deeper in shadow and the dazzle of evening sun making a mystery of sight, even of Mark's face and the dark gleam of his hair.

Perhaps this was not love; certainly not fulfilled love; he only knew it was magic, a magic with darkness in it, of which he was sometimes ashamed. But it claimed him, it shut everything else away, with an almost frightening sweetness, which, like the fast and glittering whirl of a merry-go-round, spins pleasure in the head, so that none of the muddy paths of the fairground, nor the tired people strolling there with their noisy children have relevance any more.

4

Soon after Nigel had left, Eve wrote the letter. She wrote it quickly; tore it up; then wrote it again. She put a stamp on the envelope, but didn't put the letter inside; held by indecision she left it on her desk, from which she had now removed the pages of foolscap.

Long official envelopes slipped to the mat, concerned with the Estate of James Rutherford, Deceased. These formal words combined with the incomprehensible figures which followed brought her to the verge of a panic which she knew to be exaggerated. She typed her answers carefully, pretending that they were about someone else. Then she would push it all to one side, not wishing to read 'James Rutherford, Deceased' again. I would rather, she thought, they put it some other way, for it is a word both cold and frightening: I would rather they said Killed while climbing in the Lake District.

When evening came there seemed no reason to go to bed nor to do anything with the single plate and glass from her meal nor the letters which had to be written, and she would sit, crouched on the floor, while the traffic beat like a slowing pulse outside, and voices and steps of those going to other flats sounded on the stairs.

'But there're so many things you can *do*!'

This exclamatory voice was not in her head; it came from a woman called Belinda Max, an American, wife of an Englishman who had climbed with Jamie. Belinda made jewellery and pasted dried flowers on to cardboard. She lived in a house in North London not far from the Spaniard's Inn. The house contained within its Georgian shell a gleam of modern affluence. Belinda however referred to it as the seat of her 'cottage industry'; her husband, Percy, accepted this with tolerance laced with incomprehension.

However, Belinda was truly kind, after her fashion, and indeed had the courage (which some friends had not) to enter a house of bereavement. She made several visits south to Marsham Square, driving with bewildered speed: Eve had known her comments as she manoeuvred happily up one-way streets: 'I don't understand why they're all so cross, I'm only doing my best: if people would try to *help* everything would be all right — what on earth is that little guy honking for ...?'

She arrived, bringing cold chicken, white wine and a gold decorated sprig of leaves for which it was impossible to find a vase.

She moved quickly about the flat, talking all the time; she was thin and tall, striding on long legs. Her fair hair was cut short with a fringe, her face round and snub-nosed; she wore what she called peasant dresses, long and bright-coloured: somewhere in all this was the impression of an enthusiastic child, dressed up.

'But there's so much you can *do*!' she repeated, when the golden twigs had been propped up on the mantelpiece, the chicken and wine put on the small table between them. 'You're quite young — well, not *old* — and intelligent and good-looking; a bit pale and thin now, poor darling: that's only natural; but Jamie wouldn't have wanted you to just sit and mope and think about him, now would he?'

Eve, with a piece of chicken on her fork, shook her head. This was mere politeness: she had no idea what Jamie wanted her to do now, for he was not Jamie any more.

'All you need is someone to give you that extra little push — that's right, isn't it? — and then you'll find you can get on; a little shove into the future——'

Eve said, as she'd said before, 'I don't seem to have one.'

'Now, honey, that's just nonsense. If I'm to be frank — and you'd like me to be frank, wouldn't you?'

Eve wondered absently whether anyone ever wanted to answer 'yes' to this frequent question, but Belinda went on. 'You've got so much; so much more than many other women. Why, only the other day——'

Here it came, Eve thought: the widow whose only son had been killed; the lonely woman, unmarried, who fought bravely back and was always helping someone in trouble, though she suffered from something that hurt and couldn't be cured...

Yes, yes, yes; they're all worse off than I am, and it's terrible; they stretch beyond sight, the bereaved, the lonely, the poor, the hungry, the persecuted. And I feel for them, as far as I can feel anything. But it doesn't help, it doesn't alter this grey fog: that isn't how grief works, by measurement.

'We all want to *help*,' Belinda was saying, 'but it isn't help just to sit beside you and hold your hand, is it?'

50

Eve thought perhaps it was, but this seemed no moment to disagree. One has to be so damn nice all the time, she thought; I don't know why. Belinda was going on about taking up photography, and helping the disabled and finally, after a moment of hesitation, the ultimate possibility of remarriage.

Eve listened obediently. She said, 'About remarriage——'

'Oh, I don't mean for ages: people always say two years, don't they——'

Eve went on, as if she hadn't heard. 'Just after Jamie was killed, only a few weeks later, I saw a man friend in a bookshop — he didn't see me, his back was turned, but he looked solid and masculine and full of life. And I thought — if he came out of the shop and asked me to marry him I would have said Yes, out of sheer misery.'

Belinda looked baffled, even shocked.

Eve went on with a brief smile, 'Fortunately, he didn't. Nor did anyone else, so it was just as well. Oh. . . I don't suppose I would have done really, when it came to the point. I wanted someone to take Jamie's place, to stop the silence, to stop being alone. But it wouldn't have worked. And now I feel differently.'

Belinda had found her form again. 'You have to think of all the *good* things.'

'Oh, I do.'

'All the *hopes*——'

Eve looked aside. 'I don't think I have those, except for Nigel.'

'There now, that's *wrong*. You have to hope, honey, you just have to hope, otherwise there's no life.'

Eve thought about it. 'Just now I feel there's no life.'

Belinda began again, about how much worse off other people were, and how Courage was the most important thing; and Eve listened. 'Yes,' she said; 'I'm trying hard not to be a nuisance.'

My goodness, Belinda said, she wasn't a nuisance: that wasn't the way to talk at all.

Eve received this with outward agreement, having a sense of failure, even ingratitude, that she couldn't respond more fully. She looked hopefully at Belinda, wishing to do her best. Indeed, though Belinda's words seemed to miss her attention, Eve found that she did not want her to go. When she left, the silence would return, and the knowledge that Belinda's kindness had misfired would make it no better. She said, 'I really have tried to do quite a number of things. Typing, and I go and talk to old Mrs Lake and shop for her.'

Belinda, who clearly had no idea who Mrs Lake was, said, 'That's just the sort of thing I mean. Get out among people. I know how much you must — well — miss Jamie——'

'Oh yes, I miss him.' The words had no power to convey the abyss which opened before her, but they would have to do; they were acceptable coinage. She went on, 'Of course the thing is, one ought to be able to live life backwards.'

'*Backwards?*' said Belinda, startled, as if confronted with a loss of wits.

'Yes; someone ought to tell you — while you're married, when your family's young — what it's like to be a widow.'

'Folk wouldn't listen——'

'I don't mean think about it all the time, but just to know. Have one glimpse of it, entirely as it is, only for a day. Then——'

'Then,' said Belinda with unwonted accuracy, 'you'd behave, after a fortnight, exactly as you had before.'

'I suppose so. Seems a pity.'

'You know, honey, you have to go on. You can't stay married to Jamie — no, I don't mean to be cruel — or only to be kind. You can't go on living as if everything was just the same——'

'I don't——' (But perhaps it was true.)

'You've got to think of the future.' (How the future kept coming up, Eve thought.) 'After all, you've got to think of Nigel.'

'Oh, I do. Practically all the time — in fact, I was going to ask your advice.' What extraordinary things came out of one's mouth: this wasn't true at all: she didn't want advice — or not from Belinda. 'I — I was wondering whether I ought to go and live in the country.'

It was not what she was wondering at all. Or if the idea had come into her mind as so many ideas had, it had quickly gone out again.

'Now that's the very worst thing you can do. I know how one thinks of the peace of the country and the beauty and the cows and all that. Peace instead of pace, I suppose you might say: God's peace. But believe you me, it doesn't work out that way. I've known people who've tried it — they get down there, Devonshire or Somerset or whatever it is — and then they feel *trapped*. They miss their friends, and the life-style they've known. The country isn't like it is on holiday — it can be bleak and lonely and silent. . .'

Belinda herself became silent, as if she felt her words running into the sand.

'It sounds awful,' Eve said. 'Very well, I won't go.'

Belinda looked startled, as if she'd expected resistance. 'But you said——'

'Well, yes: I'd thought of it.' (At least partly true.) 'Because sometimes I want to get out of here, and sometimes I don't want to move out of the front door, so. . .' She seemed to have lost track of what she was saying, for she perceived how this place would be when Belinda had gone, which she now realised was what she wanted her to do. 'So,' she went on, recovering herself, 'I thought I'd ask you.'

Belinda was making suggestions about holidays; her voice went on for some time, but Eve could make little sense of it. At last Belinda fell silent and Eve looked thoughtfully at the gilded branch and said, 'How kind of you to bring me that.'

Even Belinda recognised this as a signal. She sprang up and glanced round the room with penetrating vigour as if she might discover some failure which needed attention. Not finding it, save perhaps in Eve herself, she strode to the door with the long skirt swinging. 'Now you know you've only got to ring me, don't you, honey? Any time at all. Well — I suppose not right in the middle of the night, because Percy——'

No, Eve said, she wouldn't telephone in the middle of the night. She watched from the window as Belinda walked to her car. From above, the long stride seemed a caricature of itself: at once odd and endearing. To see anyone walk away, Eve thought, is a sad thing. Indeed, now that Belinda was gone Eve could remember only her kindness and her own failure to live up to it, which seemed ungracious, to be regretted, like so much else.

Returned to the room she met the silence again, emphasised by Belinda's voice and the remains of the kindly food, showing how much she had been given.

And her own letter, unposted, still remained on the table, amongst the piles of letters about James Rutherford, Deceased. The letter of which she had for a moment thought to ask Belinda's advice, and drawn back in time.

§

A few days after this she went to the wedding. The day was fine, the church at some distance, on the other side of London, far to the north, beyond Finchley. She travelled by tube, with the curious leaden surprise which at all times now accompanied her, for there seemed no reason to be travelling in this train, alone, to a wedding in which Jamie could have no part. (The bride was a daughter of his cousin, Ronald Mayne.) There were moments when she looked at the seat beside her, as if it were a new thing to find it empty. The church was large, chill, Victorian: the organ's sound banished the spaces of silence, and the bride entered with her father: tall girl with long dark hair, moving with grace towards the young man who awaited her. Now the obedient shuffle as the congregation sat or knelt or stood to sing. One more ceremony, Eve thought, such as men considered acceptable for life or death, the hiatus in time, for happiness or grief: the still moment between one life and another.

But the new life, whether of marriage or widowhood moved on, and here was the reception: the released chatter of cheerful people, the full pale glasses, the festive food. (And some echo in her mind of the room in the Rosthwaite Hotel, with the liquid sound of the beck and the dark memory of farewell.) Here was the bride, moving like some Titania between the tables, dark eyes alight, dark hair brilliant against pale skin. Eve watched her with admiration, without envy: she was too far away for that. Light bulbs flashed, adding to the confusion, for sunlight still burned outside the wide windows of the hotel. Eve lost sense of time: she seemed to have been surrounded by voices and high cheerfulness since morning, and unlikely to be free of them till night.

But soon after half-past seven the bride slid away, to return in what appeared to be a cream-coloured suit for big-game shooting. The guests drifted towards the door where the car waited. The flung dried blossom of confetti, the waving of arms, the sudden change of mood, for this was a farewell, only one of the long farewells that were to come. . .

'Goodbye. . . Goodbye. . . Good luck!'

The car moved off, the song of its wheels seeming to say *You are left behind*, and the guests, like those from whom blessing has been withdrawn, wandered back to the reception room, where the half-empty glasses and the crumby plates had the look of things abandoned.

Eve made her way home. The tube rattled mindlessly through the blank tunnels. When she came to Marsham Square, light had begun to slip from the sky, and the air which had been so bright now seemed dusted with particles of grey. Through this dust aubrietia and rose and gillyflowers burned still with bright colour. Sound travelled with peculiar clarity, and though the day had not yet gone, here and there lights showed palely at the windows. Before one house a man and woman were getting into their car. At the window above them a child stood, a boy of not more than eight years old. He stood, wearing pyjamas, his hands spread on the window-pane. The upper part of the window was open, and his voice came clearly: 'Are you going to be long?'

'No — no. A couple of hours, perhaps.'

'I don't want you to go.'

'Now come on, Jonathan; you're perfectly all right: Cathy's downstairs if you want anything.'

'I don't want Cathy, I want you.'

'Darling, we shan't be long. And you'll be asleep when we get back——'

'I shan't.'

'Now, be a good boy and go to sleep.'

'I don't want to. I shall wait up until you get back.'

The man and woman got into the car and drove off. The child didn't call any more, he still stood there and watched. Colour and grey diminishing light: danger and mystery seemed to blow through the quiet evening; some menace waited within the softly darkening road. She couldn't know the rights and wrongs of it; maybe the parents' journey was important; and anyway 'Cathy' was downstairs. . . She walked on, leaving the lighted window and the child, and the unaccountable whiff of danger.

Her room as she entered it had just enough light to see the table and chairs, dimly shining. Her letter, some days old now, lay on the table. Indecision had accompanied her in all this time: impossible to be determined about the smallest choice: what to wear, when to telephone, whether to drink coffee or tea; how to sign a letter — with love? too intimate. Sincerely? too formal. . .

But now in this twilight of early summer with the clamour of the wedding still in her head, and the child who called through the dusk, she had at least made up her mind.

§

The journey took nearly three hours. Once in the train she found that this smooth movement with strangers about her had the effect of a pacifying drug. Perhaps if one could always be in movement, from one place to another where the landscape seen from the window changed from field to town and back to field again, life would become a manageable thing. Silence was submerged beneath the noise of the train and the chatter of a woman's voice behind her: how was it that one voice always purled on and on, while some docile companion offered a Yes, No or Goodness! which was ignored. . . Had not she and Jamie laughed about it?

I mind about the jokes, she thought, almost more than anything: I wonder why? No time to consider it now; the train was slowing to its arrival, and with the end of the journey came an end of peace: the world was about her again.

She took a taxi first to the inn, where she left her case, then on to the school. The main building of Westerfield School was of Georgian grey stone, large and dignified, sitting well amongst the leafy hollow in the ground. At distances from this main building stood the separate 'houses': these were by contrast modern, square, giving the impression of a colony. The playing-fields stretched beyond the house, on higher ground. From here through the quiet air came the 'tock' of ball on cricket bat, the authentic sound of summer. She could not see from here if Nigel was playing; the white-clad figures were an anonymous company.

She went quickly into the main building of the school. An elderly man in a cardigan greeted her with the dubious deference which he no doubt allowed to all parents, and led her into a waiting-room; here copies of the *New Statesman* and *Country Life* lay on the table; she remembered that Jamie had remarked on the breadth of political interest so conveyed. . .

There must be *something*, she told herself, that doesn't make me think of him . . . but I don't know what it is. And even if I did, I should wonder what he *would* have said.

Well, that's kind of funny, she thought: you have to remember that everything, even grief, has a streak of humour: dig far enough and you find it.

After some moments the door opened as if it had been blown by blast. Larry Howard, Nigel's Housemaster, in sweat-stained shirt and green-marked flannels faced her after the enthusiasm of his entrance with a certain wariness, as if parents meant trouble. 'Sorry to keep you waiting; been taking cricket practice.' He wiped his face, which was coloured and shiny from the sun; he had a round chin, blunt nose, and though he must be forty or more, a look of eager innocence.

He led her across the grounds to his House — 'Montgomery' — (all the houses, somewhat surprisingly, were called after Generals of the First or Second World Wars). Howard's room she also remembered: filled with cricket bats, tennis racquets; silver trophies; photographs of rugger and cricket teams; on the desk an empty tea-cup and half-eaten biscuit. He swept his jacket from a chair: 'Sorry about the mess; never was one for keeping things in order — only the boys, and I can do that all right: Oxbridge may be out of favour, but when you've been a rugger blue, it counts for something, even these days. . . I got your letter.'

Simple — as if it hadn't lain for days on her table as she stayed locked in indecision.

'I thought I'd best make a date to come and see you.' As she faced him, she remembered that Jamie had said as they left, 'No wife, and I make no doubt, a life of clean living and cold baths: one way of working it out.' When she'd said working what out? Jamie had told her not to be innocent.

'About the Andorran expedition,' she said.

'Ah — yes. Going to be fun. Been there myself more than once, ski-ing. I've not been in summer before. Going to be fun,' he said again, and then his face seemed to change gear, as if he remembered. 'Well — I mean — fun for *us*.'

'I don't want Nigel to go.'

Clearly his doubts about parents had been confirmed: they only brought trouble. 'But it's all tied up! Booked. And he's looking forward to it.'

'It's too soon.'

He looked baffled, then his face changed again. 'Oh, I see. You mean after. . . But there isn't any danger, dear lady. None at all. I shall be with them, and another master, Gene Carson — young but experienced chap: very sound.'

'If there's no danger, why do you have to insure the school against accident?'

He pushed a hand through his still damp hair. Clear that any woman behaving irrationally (as she was) would at the best of times be too much for him. And this was not the best of times.

He said all schools had to insure themselves — that was routine; part of the form-filling which bedevilled our age; never had an accident; everything went like clockwork.

'Everything?'

He looked at her as he might have faced an uncertain bowler. 'Well, of course we have the odd small mishap — some silly lad treads on a broken bottle. But nothing *serious*; nothing really of the slightest consequence.'

He was looking hopefully at her, as if perhaps that settled the matter, but she went on, 'If Nigel's going could just be postponed for another year——'

'Oh ... a *year*. Well, of course, we haven't started to think about next year.' He added, 'Your husband — your late husband, I should say — was perfectly happy about it.'

'I know. But things were different then.'

He again looked baffled, confronted by this large difference. 'But if Nigel wants to go...'

She had no means of conveying to him the depth of her irrational dread. 'I know he wants to go. I've never tried to stop him — within reason — from doing anything he'd set his heart on.' (Very smug, that sounded, she thought: how good we all protest we have been, until the moment when we're being good no longer.) 'But this is something I can't help — I really can't.'

'You mean you'd withdraw your husband's permission?'

'I'm not sure. I was hoping there was some way out.'

He looked at her, she thought, with puzzled pity. 'Don't see one. Afraid it rests with you.'

She thought about it. 'I'd like to see the Head.'

His expression said, 'Oh, *Lord*,' but he himself did not. 'Terribly busy man, but I'll try.'

'I shan't keep him long.'

'Headmasters have an almost impossible job; one has to try to remember that, when they seem less than reasonable.'

As she waited in the untidy masculine room for Howard's return, she had an impulse to make a dash for the door and get the first train back to London. Both Howard and Ransome would of course judge her to be out of her mind, but that wasn't of great importance.

However, the door burst open once more; and Howard, looking both harassed and relieved, told her that Giles Ransome could see her. Yes, he'd explained what the matter was.

No chance of escape now. What on earth was she going to say to Giles Ransome who had no doubt surfaced unwillingly from a mass of paper-work and staff problems to see a rather dotty parent about Andorra? Like the mother Jamie had told her of, who

58

wrote to the Headmaster and asked if he would see *personally* that her son cooled slowly after football.

The Headmaster's room was in outstanding contrast to Howard's: no sporting trophies, no photographs of rugger teams: shelves of learned books; a desk burdened with paper and a photograph of a woman, presumably his wife. His face, lean, paler and more drawn than she remembered it, contained authority: this was different from her confrontation with Howard. After greeting her he took his glasses off and rubbed his eyes, as if he tried to get the matter into focus. 'This expedition——'

'I suppose you think I'm making a fuss about nothing.'

He put his glasses on again. 'Not exactly. When I first heard you were coming here, I thought it was to say that, for financial reasons, you'd have to withdraw Nigel from the school——'

'Oh, no! Somehow I'll keep him here: it's where he wants to be.'

'Ah . . . good. I'd certainly be sorry to lose him: he's a bright and pleasant boy.' He gave her a quick glance. 'You don't look yourself, if I may say so.'

'You mean you think I'm round the bend?'

The drift of a smile. 'No. Just that you look like someone who's come through a damaging experience.'

Oh, so that's what I look like, she thought. How odd that he should remark it.

'And because of that, you naturally fear——'

'I don't know what I fear.'

The same sigh with which perhaps he greeted a boy who gave answers wide of the mark. 'I'm not clear what you're asking me to do, Mrs Rutherford.'

No; she wasn't either, which made the whole thing more difficult. Perhaps she owed him some explanation: she would try. She said, 'When I first married Jamie, I knew nothing about climbing. (We met in a Commercial Art Studio; I was a secretary.) He only climbed on holidays and week-ends: he hadn't made his name then. I read books about mountains: Winthrop Young, Whymper and the Matterhorn, and the story of the Eiger.' She glanced at him to see if she still held his interest: his eyes were steadily on her. She went on, 'It all seemed dangerous and frightening. I asked him once to give it up — I suppose it was wrong, but I was very much in love, and I said if we were going to have a family, it wasn't fair for him to risk his life. The old argument.'

She paused again, for the words seemed out of place in this official room, but he was still listening with apparent attention.

'We talked for a long time. In the end, I knew it was no good: that he had to do it, that climbing meant life to him. I never asked him again; never said anything more. I suppose I thought, as time went on, and he was safe, that I'd done the right thing. And then ... well, you know what happened. And I've thought since, if I'd won the argument, if he'd done what I said, he'd still be alive; I'd have him with me. And now Nigel ...'

He nodded, making some mark on the blotter with his pen. 'Yes, I think I understand. But it's in our own interests, after all, to take every possible precaution. God knows, *I* don't want any trouble in the Pyrenees.'

'No.' Quite clear that he didn't. 'You're not going with them?' she asked.

'Oh, Lord — you must have heard, Mrs Rutherford, I'm not the sporting kind. That's Howard's country. It *used* to be the great tradition of the school, so when I came to take up the post of Headmaster I let Howard carry on with it, with an occasional restraining hand.' She caught a whiff of controversy; the new against the old. 'In these harsh times boys have to learn more than how to kick a ball from one end of the field to another. As to this enterprise — I daresay the experience of physical hardship comes in useful. *Any* hardship, come to that.' She saw his eyes go to the framed photograph on his desk, and had no idea what travelled through his mind. 'As to Nigel's going — I'm afraid the decision rests with you.'

'I'm not very good at decisions.'

His eyes went broodingly over her face, perhaps to remind himself that she had excuse for wasting his time. 'If you want to withdraw your husband's permission, we'll have to get another boy to take his place. Not difficult, I daresay, but of course there's the question of cash — quite a large question in these days. Nigel's payment has already been made.'

'I know.'

'So we'll need to know soon.'

'Yes. There's just one more thing——'

He propped his chin on his hand, as if he needed support.

She said, 'This friendship with Mark Stevens——'

'Oh — that. We keep an eye on it.'

'Then you *do* think——'

'Nothing serious. Mark's a boy of strong personality, and

60

parents with more money than most. Friendships with such boys
are frequent. But not more than friendship — with perhaps, let's
say, that flavour of romance which is inseparable from all young
life.'

She nodded, having said all she could. Nothing to do but go.
She got to her feet. 'I'll tell you as soon as I can. Thank you for seeing me.'

He made a small gesture of acknowledgement, perhaps of sympathy. 'You'll want to see Nigel, now you're here.'

Impossible to say she did not. Untrue, for he was life as
opposed to death. But now . . . She said she would, and found herself back in the waiting-room, with the *New Statesman* and *Country Life*, as if this visit had come full circle.

When Nigel came in, he looked vaguely startled and said, 'Gosh
— hullo, Ma — what's wrong?'

'Nothing, darling. I — I simply wondered if you could get permission to come out to dinner this evening. I'm staying at the inn.'

'This evening?' He looked doubtful. 'I've got an awful lot of
prep. Howard's had us on the cricket field all the afternoon, and
with exams coming up. . .'

The question as to why she was there at all remained between
them. You didn't just drop in on Derbyshire from London for a
possible evening out. While she tried to think of what best to say,
Mark came into the room.

'Oh — sorry,' he said. 'Didn't know you were here, Mrs Rutherford.' (Didn't he? She wasn't sure.) 'Nigel's supposed to be swot-
ting himself blue on maths. Someone told me he was here——'

She saw a glance go between them.

She explained about the question of dinner. It would, of
course, be polite to ask Mark to come too, but she did not. He
leaned against the wall and said, 'Not for me to say, but they're
putting a bit of pressure on us; you know what exams are. Personally I'm not all that bothered: one of my ancestors must have had
a photographic memory and I can *see* the page of the textbook.'

After a small silence, Nigel blurted out, 'Did you come about
the Andorran thing?'

Before she could answer Mark said with a touch of irony, 'The
Andorran adventure. Quite fun, in a simple way.'

She said, 'Yes, I came about that.'

Mark shifted himself from the wall. 'I'll leave you to it, then.'

When he had gone Nigel said, 'What did you say?'

61

'I asked questions.'

Nigel sat down. 'You didn't put the lid on it, did you?'

'No. I told Ransome I'd let him know.'

'You mean you haven't decided?'

'No.'

'That's not fair. I want to know. If you're going to say I can't go, say it now.'

She had not for a long time heard such hostility in his voice. All right, she told herself: if this hurts, it's your own fault. She said, 'I don't want to disappoint you. Truly I don't.'

'Well, then——'

'If Mark wasn't going, would it be so important?'

Colour came to his face. 'I don't know. . . Did you say anything about Mark, just now?'

'Why should I?'

'Don't know. Because I suppose you never seem to get on with him.'

'I've always made him welcome!' What absurd formal phrases one used when one wasn't telling the truth.

'Yes, I suppose. But — I never felt happy when I brought him home.'

'I'm sorry.' Further and further into the places of misgiving and pain, but still hampered from getting free of them. 'It's true I've always felt a bit awkward with him, I don't know why. Ransome said his parents were pretty well-off——'

'So you did talk about him?'

'I mentioned him, yes. I — I thought if Mark could be sure of going next year, then you might be resigned to going too.'

'He can't go next summer. He told me, he's going to the States. His father's got some sort of business do on, and they're going for the whole summer. New York, and then right over to the West Coast — California. It sounds marvellous.'

'You'd like to go with them?'

'Oh — it just isn't on. . . Nobody's asked me. Who'd pay, anyway?'

No, she couldn't pay for a trip to the States: not as well as keeping him at school. There remained Andorra. She said, 'You're sure you can't make dinner?'

'There's the work.'

'Yes, I see.' Indeed she did, for in other circumstances he would have made an effort to come.

'Where are you going now?'

'To the inn for the night. Then . . . home.'

He faced her, baffled, at odds. A need to bring the barrier down, to let the strangled love go free kept her still, but silent. He said, 'I'm sorry, but it's only for two weeks. I just don't see. . .'

No, of course he didn't. And no use to protest further. She walked away, wondering if this were to be in the country of unreason. If so, it had to be accepted; perhaps later fought.

She looked back at him once, as he stood on the steps of the school house. At this distance, a manner of stance, some posture of the head, resembled his father. She lifted a hand, to which he half-heartedly replied.

I'm making a mess of this, she told herself: I've got it wrong. Jamie would have known what to do.

She thought as she walked back to the inn, I need help. I don't want to be a nuisance, but I need help because Jamie isn't here any more, and without him I'm getting everything wrong.

The inn was astir with life. What an extraordinary thing to have done, she thought: written to the school, and talked to the Housemaster and Headmaster, as if on some matter of great moment.

She thought, I need to get out of here.

It was half past six. There was still time to get a return train to London. All at once she felt a longing to be back in the London home: there was a sensation, not of course believed (as she had told Nigel) that Jamie would be waiting for her, or some residue of his strength.

She could catch the seven-fifteen train with luck — there was still her bill to pay. The young man at the reception desk became bothered about the bill and began to search for a ledger. 'You booked to stay the night, madam.'

'I know; I have to return unexpectedly.'

'I'm afraid we have to charge——'

'I don't mind what you charge! I just want to get the seven-fifteen.'

He glanced at the clock. 'Cutting it fine——'

'I know. That's why I want to pay my bill, and I want a taxi——'

'I can only do one thing at a time, madam——'

'It doesn't matter about the bill; I'll give you a blank cheque——'

He looked at her with wounded reproach. 'I'm afraid that wouldn't do at all——'

'Then please *hurry*——'

'I'm doing my best, madam.'

She had time to feel sorry for him, confronted with one of those visitors who muddled the even tenor of management.

As she paid her bill she heard a taxi drive up. Crying, '*Hold* it,' to the surprise of the new visitors, she thrust her suitcase into the cab. 'Station, please; I want to catch the seven-fifteen.'

'Running it fine,' the driver said.

'Please.'

'Do my best.'

He drove at speed, so fast she wondered if they would arrive at the station at all. It was odd to feel the occasional shaft of fear, for what did it matter, after all?

The station now. Scrambling, fumbling with her purse (surprising how clumsy she had become at all times now) she grabbed her suitcase and ran.

§

It was as he went quickly down the corridor of 'Montgomery' that Nigel met Mark with a pile of books under his arm. Though burdened with school books, Mark had an air of detachment from them, as if he merely transferred them from one place to another.

'Hullo,' Mark said, 'got skates on?'

Nigel put his hands in his pockets. This seemed to be a day when he was in the wrong part of the court, whatever happened. He said, 'I'm going to the inn. I've got per. from Howard. I'm going to have dinner with Ma.'

'Oh. . . Lord. I thought we'd got that all tied up.'

'So we have. I just thought I'd go and have dinner. She wanted me to come.'

'Well, sure she did. But it only means more pressure; you know that.'

Nigel looked at the floor. 'I don't think so. I think she's got the message. I just feel I ought to be there.'

'It's a fool's game.'

Stubbornness entered him. 'I don't think so. I think it's best to go. Be sort of nice to her.'

'You know how it'll end.'

Nigel shook his head. 'I've made up my mind. About Andorra. But she went away . . . well, we said goodbye without anything.

Cold. You know what I mean.'

'She'll get over it.'

'Maybe. But I want to go.'

Mark looked at him with one eyebrow lifted. 'O.K., I'm not stopping you. But don't say you haven't been warned.'

Nigel went quickly into the warm quiet evening. To go out of school at unaccustomed hours always had the feel of adventure. Perhaps all formal patterns of life, even when they were accepted and enjoyed, carried within them the contrary desire to escape, to be alone as he was now, going quickly on his errand.

As he looked back he could see the school, with the silken green of trees about it; from here it looked like a place of extreme calm. It was familiar as hands and feet, yet it came to him suddenly that in two years' time he would be leaving it forever. So nothing was permanent, nothing stable: where would Mark be then?

The entrance to the inn was familiar also: the civilized rendezvous where boys came to be given large teas or luncheons of roast beef, and puddings on a trolley with all the colours of a flower show . . .

He went with confidence to the reception desk. He was glad he'd come: not always certain of himself, never as sure as Mark, he had the sense of a knot coming untied. The lamp-lit pages at home still haunted him: it would be better to see her. He said to the young man behind the desk, 'I've come to see my mother. Mrs Rutherford.'

'Mrs Rutherford . . .? Yes, she booked a room, but I'm afraid she's gone.'

'But she was staying the night!'

Faint weariness touched the young man's face. 'She decided to return at once to London. She intended to catch the seven-fifteen train.'

'But——' Nigel began; the young man gave a small dismissive smile and turned to a woman who also waited at the desk. Nigel stood for a moment bewildered; his mother's absence had the total surprise of a missing stair. The seven-fifteen train? He glanced at the clock: a quarter to eight. The train had already gone, was already eating the miles of the familiar journey——

The young man at the desk turned for a moment. 'I suppose she caught it; she must have cut it pretty fine.'

Nigel nodded. Cutting it fine. Perhaps she'd missed the train? There wasn't another for two hours: he knew the timetable well enough, and he could see the waiting-room which like most small station waiting-rooms seemed to be a cross between a school-room and a mortuary... He'd been given the evening off; what best to do?

He found he was on his way to the station. The walk, if some distance, was downhill; the evening air sleepily warm. He had a picture in his mind of his mother in the waiting-room, with nearly two hours ahead of her. As he walked he had a sense of well-doing — already he could imagine how glad she would be to see him, how they would return to the inn, with the old friendliness, to have dinner. He'd say nothing more about Andorra; for the present that was best left alone.

The station. The new British Rail sign an anachronism on the soured brick of the Victorian façade. Scraps of paper blowing over the stone floor; Nigel went quickly through the dark tunnel and up the iron steps to the platform for the London train. He was already planning the words in his head as he passed the posters adrift from the wall. . .

He looked into the waiting-room. Exactly as he remembered it, a dirge of a place, with flaking walls, and an empty grate where perhaps in past years a fire had burned. But empty. No sign of his mother, nor of anyone, since no train was expected for a long time. He came out of the waiting-room and looked up and down the platform. The shining empty iron road of the track, the signals at red. Nothing and no one there. He sat on one of the station seats. His heart was going fast, and he became aware that this was because he was angry. Reasonlessly, powerfully angry. He'd come all this way, he'd seen himself as some kind of knight errant; he'd lost the whole evening, come finally to this desert of a station, made emptier by the low sunlight which gleamed on it, from which his mother had left for London, now nearly an hour ago.

He strode back, still charged with anger, to the school. Glad to find it again, he went into the garden of his House, for supper would be over, and some of the boys out there in the fine, dwindling day.

Mark was lying on the grass, propped on one elbow, talking to two other boys. Mark had a habit, Nigel reflected, remembering Lynton Boyle, of talking to people with casual ease when one wanted him most. He went up to them, and Mark, shading his eyes against the sun, said, 'Back so soon? That was a fast meal.'

'I drew it in with a straw. I'd like a word with you.'

Mark rose without haste and wandered with Nigel to the end of the garden. If glances followed them, Nigel did not care. 'She's gone,' he said. 'Back to town.'

'No splendid dinner at the inn?'

'No dinner at all. I went to the station——'

'To the *station*? What a thundering bore.'

'And I know what *this* means,' Nigel said. 'She's made up her mind. She's going to say no.'

'You reckon?'

'I'm sure.' He kicked at the grass. Anger and the rapid walk had made his breath come more quickly. 'That's why she's gone. So's not to have to see me again. The next thing I'll know is a summons from Howard, and the whole thing'll be off.'

They were at the far end of the garden. Mark put an arm across Nigel's shoulders. 'Might be all right,' he said.

'I wanted to go. It's only for a fortnight. Why the hell shouldn't I?' He had quite lost the image of his mother, alone in the waiting-room; lost even those lamp-lit and guilty pages: she was off on the train's canter to London, to a different world. Perhaps it was just the confusion of this day, the scene with his mother, the long walk to the station, the mixture of pity and anger, but he felt his eyes sting and saw the grass blur.

'Plenty of summer left,' Mark said; 'plenty of time.'

The school clock rang through the warmth and softening light. Mark's hand strengthened on his shoulder.

5

Eve decided that there was one more thing to do, made a telephone call and found herself at Liverpool Street Station. (Perhaps I could write about this, she thought, and call it 'An Experience of Stations'). Who had once said that *angst* was worst at Waterloo? Liverpool Street had an absence of cheer, an awkward shape as if it were crowded into an unwelcome corner.

Nevertheless the sliding of the train worked its usual balm: she sat like a child provided with entertainment which only peripherally catches its attention: the tower blocks, the anonymous streets, the green lakes of land . . .

One more arrival; the world again. Norwich Station she found a sight more welcoming than Liverpool Street. Jamie's father was waiting by his car and he greeted her with something near warmth. 'I hoped you'd come.'

She felt guilty, remembering how long his letter of invitation had lain unanswered on her desk. 'I'm sorry. There's been so much business, things like that——' In her mind's eye she saw the pile of letters, referring to James Rutherford, Deceased.

'Oh, there's no need to apologise.' She glanced at his profile as he looked above the wheel of the car. It was like meeting someone well known but not seen for many years. She couldn't gauge his mood, nor tell from this view what changes the last months had worked on him. 'Just that I'm glad to see you. I'm sure Jamie would have wished it . . . *does* wish it.'

This had not occurred to her: Jamie . . . *now*?

She made an effort to encompass this unimaginable prospect. When they came to the Vicarage, she looked at it as if it were a new place. The recent sun, as always, had deserted it: the trees, chestnut and fir, leaned close, weaving their shadow.

He had put her in a single room, not the room she had shared with Jamie. She didn't know if this sprang from necessity or consideration, but she was glad of it. When she came downstairs she found him in the living-room. Shadowed, as she remembered it, but she could see her father-in-law more clearly now.

Why, he looks old! she thought. He must of course be over seventy, but he had walked always upright, his hair grey. Now the hair was white, the pate almost bald, and his shoulders a little bent. Every now and again he straightened them, as if he had been reminded to. 'You'd like some sherry?' he asked. 'I'm afraid it's not very good, but that's due to forces beyond my control — the Government, and the upkeep of this house ... Oh! please don't think you're not welcome: it's just that things become a little shabby and one buys the second-rate.'

She had not expected to feel pity for him, who had always commanded. 'Where's your housekeeper ... what's her name? Mrs Brooks.'

'I'm afraid she had to go, along with the better sherry. She's married again and living — happily, as far as I know — in Frodsham.'

'So you're here alone?'

He straightened his shoulders. 'No need to worry about that; I'm used to it. I have a woman from the village who comes and cleans——' (Not very well, Eve thought, as she glimpsed the dust on the surfaces of table and desk) — 'and makes a form of pie or some such for me before she goes home. It's perfectly adequate — indeed, I'm quite glad to have the place to myself.'

Possibly this was true, but she couldn't rid herself of pity, which was a new thing. (*Jamie would have been pleased that you've come* ... was it so? One could be sure of nothing, of course.)

With his glass, he sat down opposite her. 'You're still not yourself, are you?'

'I don't know what myself is.'

'No ... no, few of us, I suppose, truly know that. But I've seen — naturally — so many die in the course of my ministry, and so many of the bereaved: one gets to know the look, as a doctor gets to know the symptoms of a disease.' The grey summer evening lost further light. He said, 'I wonder whether you want to talk about Jamie.'

'Oh yes, I want to talk about him. All the time. But mostly I feel people don't want to, and I'm afraid of boring them.'

Clyde Rutherford took a sip of his sherry. 'When Jamie's mother died I didn't want to talk. People said such foolish things. But Jamie — yes, like you I wanted to talk about him. Perhaps for different reasons ... Of course, you may think it too late — or the wrong time — to go back, over the years.'

'No, I don't think so.'

He looked aside. 'As one gets older, one wants to explain. So much of the past one would like to alter——'

Yes, she said; only recently she'd told a woman friend that she'd thought life ought to be lived backwards.

'Ah! indeed. But what's done's done. I was very proud of Jamie, you know, when he was a boy. He was extremely intelligent and so good-looking — he got his looks from his mother, needless to say. I used to observe other children who had so much less, and feel a tremendous and I suppose quite un-Christian pride. I've done my job as a parson as best I can, but I'm no saint — never have been. Too ready a temper, and a marked aversion to anyone who opposed my ideas.' He looked at her over his glass with a wry smile. 'You'll remember that perhaps.'

This seemed to be a time for truth. She said, 'Yes.'

'As he grew up I wanted him to be my disciple, as he had been as a child. But of course he had his own opinions. Not an uncommon problem, but I took it badly.' Again he looked aside to the shadows of the room. 'Poor Marjorie had a difficult time keeping the peace between us — I see that now. No use brooding on it. I didn't so much shout as use sarcasm. A nasty weapon and certainly not a Christian one. But one tends to use the weapon easiest to hand.'

She watched him with devoted attention, her own question temporarily forgotten. This was Jamie's father, speaking as he had not done before. He went on, 'Jamie was keen on art, and I've never had much taste for it. And then climbing. . . I've never been much interested in sports, either. (You may ask, What *do* I like? Oh, theological books, philosophy . . . The occasional biography, when I take pleasure in the fall of the subject, I'm afraid, rather than his rise.) I just felt this business of climbing about rocks was such a waste of time. I wanted so much for him. . .' He glanced at her. 'Would you like the light on? It's a dull day.'

She shook her head. This encounter in the dusty and shadowed room had the element of discovery. Was this because she was talking to Jamie's father: did the blood connection — as with Nigel — create some sort of ease?

'So we argued,' he said. 'Yet all the time, I hoped for great things for him. And when Marjorie died, so many years ago . . . I hoped even more. I couldn't expect to leave him anything much in the way of money, but he seemed to have such gifts. I hoped that perhaps he'd become a don — and (I must be honest) that he'd marry, not wealth necessarily but standing, if that's the word. I trust you understand.'

'Of course.'

'I didn't feel — you'll forgive me — that you were the right person for him. Or what *I* thought to be the right person. Of course I can see now that nothing would stop Jamie from climbing, and nothing would stop his marrying you. Please don't be distressed——'

'I'm not.' Nor was she. For the first time in a long while she was absorbed, even brought to some sort of life: perhaps truth, in these times, became a friend.

'I was I suppose, blinded by my hopes. Had it not been so, I might have got to know you, found common ground——'

'I can see quite clearly,' she said. 'I was an untidy and scatter-brained girl whose father had left home for good (if that's the word) and with a mother who was adrift in her mind. I had no money and no "standing" as you call it: I had nothing——'

'Except of course fine looks, and Jamie's love.'

Odd, the things that trapped you. She turned her head away, so that he should not see.

'I didn't want to believe that you were — I won't say the one person for Jamie, because only God can say that — but the best as the world goes.' He gave her a brief glance, but perhaps the shadows in the room hid her face from him. 'However, now I look back, I wish I *had* known you. Will that do as an apology? I'm not much used to making them, as you will remember.'

'I don't think I need apologies. There seem to be such a lot of things you don't need any more.'

He nodded, and levered himself up, hands on the arms of his chair. 'I'll get the prepared meal — no, don't move. If I want to be polite I say that I like my guests to sit at ease, and if I tell the truth that I prefer the kitchen to myself. Take another glass of sherry — yes, yes, I insist; things aren't as bad as that.'

She sat alone in the room, hearing him in the kitchen across the hall. An unexpected peace contained her, which was not happiness but was of a different colour from the time till now.

The doorbell startled her, for this had seemed to be a time shut out from the world. He arrived from the kitchen, removing a man's apron. 'How extraordinary — like the telephone, isn't it? Always when one's in the bath or dishing up.' He flung the apron on to a chair, with an impatience which recalled his earlier self, a man without much time for circumstances that thwarted him.

Hearing voices in the hall, she hoped that this privacy was not to be invaded.

The woman who came into the room was perhaps fifty, and cancelled her hope. She clearly found Eve a doubtfully welcome surprise.

Clyde said, 'You know my daughter-in-law?'

The new face, not recovered from surprise, said, 'I don't think we've met.'

'Not? Eve, this is Mrs Vaughan. Mrs Valerie Vaughan.'

Eve looked at Mrs Vaughan. Pretty, putting on weight, hair distorted and blonded by some trained hand; a dress of petunia pink which showed up oddly in the vicarage room. She sat with a little plump on a chair. The sound, though quiet, had something determined about it. 'Then I won't stay long. But as I'm here, I'm sure Mrs Rutherford will forgive me if I just say a word or two.'

Possibly, Eve thought, Mrs Rutherford would: she was not so sure about her father-in-law. Clyde, drumming the fingers of one hand on the back of a chair, glanced towards the kitchen (from which came a smell of cooking) with controlled impatience. Mrs Vaughan spoke of volunteers for brass cleaning, for the summer bazaar; the organization of the Stewardship Campaign. She offered a sheaf of papers which Clyde accepted with a rapid glance. 'Thank you. Very kind.' He drew one hand over thinning hair. 'I forget myself. Won't you have some sherry?'

Something less than enthusiasm in this question seemed to reach Mrs Vaughan. She rose from the chair, and pulled at the creases in her pink skirt. 'I'll come another time.' She gave Clyde an embracing smile and a little tap on his arm. 'No one can say I'm one of those who outstays her welcome, can they, Clyde?' Not waiting for an answer she said goodbye to Eve and made for the door.

Clyde returned. His lean face showed the dry smile of a man who has won a battle, perhaps not with honour. When he had laid the meal on the table, he said, 'This is a fish-pie, I believe; we shall soon discover . . . I'm sorry we were interrupted.'

'Yes, so was I.'

'You didn't care for Valerie Vaughan?'

'I didn't have time. . .'

Clyde wiped his mouth and said, 'Would it surprise you to know that she'd like to marry me? — Yes, I see it would.'

'*Marry?*'

'Not for any grace or beauty — or even wealth — that I possess, as you can see. And I've had my three score and ten; more must be a decline. But Valerie was widowed some five years ago. You may wonder why she didn't marry again——'

'No,' Eve said; 'I would never wonder about anyone not marrying again.'

'Ah — well, now she makes it clear in many small ways that she would like to be, shall we say, the lady of the vicarage.'

She tried to view Mrs Vaughan in this new light. 'But——'

'You're going to say she'd drive me mad. Yes, she would.'

'Then——'

'Oh, I've no intention of giving in. (Does that sound presumptuous? You'll have to take my word that the hints have been as broad as a church door, and that among my parishioners it's something of a standing joke.) I suppose a Vicar, though without youth, looks, or even a particularly nice nature has a certain prestige, even in these times — anyway, he has in a village like this.'

'I can see that.'

'How restful: you see a great deal. No, I resist, and shall——'

'Resist?'

A wry smile. 'I take the sacrament to many old people's homes. I did so the other day. The old sit there — some not quite in their right mind; some alert, but unable to move. It *has* occurred to me that a younger wife would tend such a one more carefully — do I shock you?'

'Nothing shocks me any more.'

'Good. But of course the price would be too high. As you say — or rather didn't say — she would drive me mad. Are you enjoying your pie?'

'Yes, I think so. Food tastes different.'

'It may be that since Jamie's death she's come to believe — well, it's true — that I'm more vulnerable.'

She glanced at him, remembering the moment by the Borrowdale graveside when she had been jealous of any grief but her own. Now she felt the shaft of comradeship.

He went on, having eaten a forkful of pie, 'To lose a son — an only son — even if you've not got on too well with him, is a dark thing. Oh, I make no claims (if that's the word) to the kind of grief which you know. But it is contrary to nature, to grow old and see a son die. The world loses proportion: death which one expects to see on the road ahead, comes up from behind. Yes, in my own way, I've known grief, not less because of the long absences and anger. So suddenly, there's no more time.'

'I know.'

'So you see, I am bereft. And she is lonely, of course.'

The word didn't seem to apply to the busy pink lady with her many plans. 'She seemed ... so *busy*.'

'Indeed. Never stops. Meetings, telephone calls, coffee mornings, church fellowships, concerts... But all done, I think, because of loneliness ... it takes people different ways.'

'Have I got to be sorry for her?'

'No more than for anyone — no more or less.'

She thought, Perhaps he will marry her, after all. Nothing was certain; death untied boundaries, and the world was open. Lifting her head, she heard the tumbled sound of church bells.

'Bell-ringers' practice,' he said. 'Know anything about it? Quite interesting: a chap called Steadman wrote a book about it in the seventeenth century; I've got it somewhere on the shelves. You wouldn't believe how much there is to know. This is quite a simple exercise; we have six bells, and they're ringing the changes.' He listened as the heavy yet musical sound travelled the evening air, carried on a rising wind. As if the sound had brought memory to him he said, 'When we spoke at Jamie's funeral I had the impression that you had no intention of coming to see me——'

'I'm afraid that's true. After all——'

'We'd not been close. I know.'

'I suppose when Jamie was alive it was all simple. We had friends, but it didn't really *matter* if we didn't see them. If we didn't see anybody — except Nigel, of course. And sometimes I think we didn't see enough of *him*. Marriage, if it's all right, is a kind of buffer; you travel in a train carriage, and you see people as you pass by. It was easy — too easy, perhaps — to forget about you.'

'Naturally.'

'It's all different now, of course. One sees people in quite another perspective. Important; sometimes, God knows, exhausting. But — needed.'

The ageing eyes, creased and intelligent, looked kindly on her. 'Yes, indeed. That's why I hoped you'd come. I was ... aware of you; you might say, curious. For after all, the death of one's partner makes a new person——'

'Or no person at all.'

'Ah, yes; in your case — perhaps of most women — it seems like that. But the new person is there, waiting to emerge. Especially for someone no older than you.'

'I don't feel any age. Not young, not old, not even middle-aged. I seem to be nothing to do with time.'

'Well, in a sense one isn't, of course. My faith has stood pretty well, over the years. Who was it said of hope "God has saved this good wine till last?" I think it's true. Time is man's concept, not God's. It may be something like that you're feeling now. You may not know it.'

'I don't think I do.'

'You will, I believe. As I say, I've had much experience of people's grief. They react in the most unlikely ways. A man I know — suddenly widowed — not only went round the world, but danced every night till three while he did it. Yet he was most stricken. Of course he was lucky to be *able* to go round the world.'

'No, I don't want to do that. The world doesn't taste of anything.'

The eyes were still on her. 'You haven't, I hope, a total despair of life?'

It was easy to talk like this in the darkening room. Outside, the sound of the bells still beat on the moist air. 'I suppose I have had. Even now, I sometimes think it would be a solution. One wouldn't have to wake up any more, to try. It would answer everything, except. . .'

He waited, silent, hands crossed under his chin.

'Except Nigel.'

He nodded. 'The boy. There again — my only grandchild . . . and I don't know him. Oh, you don't have to explain. If I was at a distance from you, how much more from him. My own fault. But . . . let me show you something. It may help you.' He rose from the table, searched in a drawer of a desk, returned with a book. 'Here . . . you see?' It was an album, with the first photographs carefully mounted, the later ones loose. He said, 'Marjorie used to take great care, as you see; I meant to, and never seemed to have time.'

She looked with intent interest. The early photographs showed Jamie as a child, as a young man. She thought How confident and unknowing youth is: there's no thought of death on that face, no acknowledgement of it, even. She could not take her eyes away. 'But here,' he said, 'the order stops . . . nevertheless, I keep them, sometimes look at them, at these pictures of Nigel as a child. . .

Perhaps you're surprised?'

Yes, she was. ' We used to send them, always — I never knew if you really wanted them.'

'Oh, yes, I wanted them. And after Jamie died, more than ever. For I looked at these pictures of Nigel and thought There is something still living; everything has not died.'

'You felt that too?'

'Oh, yes. I've been no better a grandfather than a father. The threshold of my patience is low. But that doesn't prevent me from taking nourishment at the thought of Jamie's son.'

'If you'd like to see him——'

'Ah yes; some time. But don't expect too much. I daresay it's too late to make up for lost years. If one's not dug and nurtured and weeded, one can't expect the garden to grow.'

'I'll try to bring him. Just now there's a question.'

He listened. Absently he turned a page of the book while she told him of the Andorran expedition.

'As you can imagine this sort of thing makes no appeal to me. However — you say he wants to go? ... Yes ... And you're afraid?'

'It seems to be something larger than that. I dream about it; I'd give anything to hear that for some reason they'd had to call the whole thing off. I can see that what they all say is reasonable — if Jamie hadn't been killed, I wouldn't have thought twice. He'll be safe enough. And yet...'

He looked as if he were pondering the 'and yet'. 'I think I understand. It *feels* wrong to you, in spite of all the things people say.' She nodded. He went on, 'But ... thinking of the past, I must say: let him go.'

She had not expected that the words would in the first moments bring relief: perhaps the end of any conflict eases the mind, she thought, even if it is the end you don't want. Very well; she would abide by his word.

He said, 'You see, in the end, it will be better. If you refuse him there'll be a division between you, just as there was between Jamie and myself. If I could go back, I'd do differently; I'd try to be with him in spirit.'

'In spite of what's happened?'

He nodded slowly. 'Yes — in spite even of that.'

Though some relic of fear still persisted, she knew that a decision had been made. She became silent. What had changed in the room? Nothing; only the light, because Clyde had lit the table lamp, making the garden beyond a void of darkness. Yet she was aware now of difference; of some vanished quiet.

She said, 'Can you turn on another light?'

6

Larry Howard, Nigel thought, was perhaps as much in his element as he would ever be. He was — together with Gene Carson — in charge of a dozen boys, on his way to the Pyrenees. Just now they had reached Perpignan, after a flight which had been delayed because of air congestion over France. 'Boring,' Mark had observed while they waited, 'but better than crashing into the frogs.' Outside Howard was counting the boys, which he would go on doing throughout the trip. The day was cloudy. A coach waited, a piratical driver at the wheel, anxious it seemed to be off. Gene Carson spoke to him in Spanish; the driver flung away a strong-smelling cigarette and sat hunched over the wheel with his head down, as if praying for help.

Nigel followed Mark into the coach. Well, this was France, and they were on their way to the mountains; it was an adventure, though it did not yet feel like one.

Once they were in the coach, Gene Carson picked up a microphone which exploded into life with the noise of a firecracker. Gene regulated it and said, 'Our driver tells us that as we're more than an hour late, it'll be dark by the time we get to the appointed place in Andorra. He also says that the drive is long — and as far as I can make out from his Spanish which is unconventional — high and hazardous. As we travel from sea-level to something like nine thousand feet, this goes without saying. Miguel, our driver, says Do not be ashamed if you shut your eyes as we take the sharpest bends in the road; he does the same. I guess this is a joke. If any of you feel sick, for God's sake tell us in time. I doubt if we can stop on a mountain bend, but your fellow travellers can at least get out of the way.'

He handed the microphone to Howard, and folded his long legs into a front seat. He had the casual air of a world sailor prepared for a trip round the harbour. By contrast Howard was full of fluster and life and, Nigel thought, not best pleased that Gene Carson was the one who could speak in foreign tongues.

Howard's voice came with deafening vigour; he too adjusted

the microphone with impatience, and said, 'As soon as we get to our camping place, we put up our tents. Won't be so easy by torch-light, but all the better practice. Worse things happen on the Eiger. No one left anything behind? . . . O.K.: That's it, then: now for Andorra.'

The coach lurched forward; Larry Howard fell into place and the boys bounded on hard seats. Light rain began to fall, and the far shape of the Pyrenees ahead of them faded to nothing.

Mark said to Nigel, 'They say this is going to take five hours.'

Nigel didn't reply. The rain increased. He told himself again that this was France, they were bound for the unknown country of Andorra, his mother had given the all-clear, and Mark was beside him. Yet the mist and the shining and serpentine road gave him a twinge of apprehension, as if somewhere along the line there had been an important and now irreversible error.

§

Eve accepted the invitation of Mr and Mrs Rufus Stevens to stay for the week-end as she accepted much else, without conscious thought. Week-ends in strangers' houses had never been a habit of Jamie: he'd said that you never knew when you could have a bath and no one gave you a drink when you wanted one and they talked at *breakfast*, of all things.

Nigel had left for his Andorran expedition two days ago. His acceptance of her decision had been a little guarded: natural enough, perhaps. The silence in the flat after she had said goodbye to him had contained for a little while the threat of the silence in those first weeks after Jamie's death. But now she accepted that Nigel was away, enjoying himself, and the two weeks would, for her, quickly pass. Her protests, her efforts to prevent his going seemed now like an aberration.

She had made a fool of herself, that was all. Her only excuse was the memory which would not leave her, of the day of the climb, of the hospital and the end of it all. This had taken joy from life, as a surgeon removes an organ from the body.

Oh yes, she said to the person who kept up a monitoring argu-ment in her head; I know the world is a fine and sometimes beauti-ful place; I know I have what is loosely called my health and strength, but whatever the spring of joy is, wherever its root lies, I haven't got it any more. Except in Nigel. I don't say I may not find it again, for I can see that nothing is impossible: if life can over-turn so suddenly as it did with Jamie's death, it can, I suppose, overturn again.

It was autumn now. An element of discovery here, for it would be the first autumn alone. On the journey to the Stevens she looked with curiosity at the colours of yellow and bronze, and the ragged autumn flowers in gardens as they passed. A new time, a new season . . . What did that remind her of? Something Jamie had quoted often; for Jamie, though he went to no church, was, as he reminded her, a parson's son, and ancient words were part of his heritage . . . 'Though in the ways of fortune or misunderstand-ing, or conscience, thou have been benighted till now, wint'red and frozen, clouded and eclipsed, damp and benumbed, smothered and stupefied till now, now God comes to thee, not as in the dawn-ing of the day, not as in the bud of the spring, but as the sun at noon, to banish all shadows; as the sheaves in harvest, to fill all penuries. All occasions invite His mercies, and all times are His seasons . . .' Was it true? She had no means of knowing; yet the words, learned by heart long ago because Jamie cared so much for them, had returned accurately to her mind.

One more arrival, in a soft Autumn sun. So this was where Nigel came to stay with Mark . . . and this was Mark's father who, though she hadn't met him, was clearly identifiable. As he greeted her she could see a trace of that young yet world-weary face, even in this man of middle-age who was putting on weight. But his man-ner was different, cheerful, competent, unstriving. 'It's only a step to the house,' he said, taking her suitcase; 'not worth bringing the car, unless it's raining.' The country lane was quiet, the fields rich with harvest. 'I wonder if you'll like the house,' he added; 'swim-ming-pool and such. My wife's idea: she likes things like that. But it may not be your kind of thing.'

She was surprised at his concern. Did she perhaps not look to be the kind of person who would like a swimming-pool? Possible, since she wore a tunic and trousers some years old. She tried to reassure him by saying that Nigel had always enjoyed himself there.

'Oh — yes; well, the young enjoy themselves in most places, don't they? I came from what I can now see was a pretty cheerless Victorian street in West London, but I saw nothing wrong with it at the time. My father was a small shopkeeper, a newsagent. I'll tell you that now, as my wife doesn't like to hear me say so.'

80

It appeared he was a friend. A rather stumpy man, walking with none of his son's grace beside her, yet conveying a touch of comradeship. He went on, 'Laura and Mark enjoy luxury: I don't. If I hadn't a family, I often think I'd give it all up, and go and live in a croft. Or on a barge.'

'Really? I've had leanings towards a croft myself. Of course I shall never go there.'

A sideways glance. 'One can understand — about the croft, I mean. I've thought of you, sometimes——'

'But we've never met!'

'Nigel has spoken of you. I've thought how it would be, to be suddenly alone.'

How had he found time amongst all those accounts and economic crises to think of a widow whom he had never met? . . . He would not, however, wish for a long description of the last months, even if she could have given one. She said, 'One can't explain. You don't know who you are; one bit of you is missing. I had migraine once; half my vision blacked out. It's rather like that.'

'Nasty,' he said.

'I suppose it is. You come to accept it. That's how things are.'

'I guess so. Would it embarrass you if I told you you were being brave?'

'*Brave*? Oh, goodness, no. I mean, I'm not. I put one foot in front of the other. Anyone can do that. I cry and cry and at times I behave like the White Rabbit. That's not brave.'

They had reached the house. Prepared for a meeting with the Stevens only, she was surprised to see Giles Ransome with his wife; and a stranger called Henry Boyle, with his son, Lynton. (Mrs Boyle appeared to be absent.) Giles Ransome had the odd appearance of a man seen out of context: she had never met him beyond the confines of the school. Julia Ransome, a tall good-looking woman with dark hair parted in the middle and drawn back tightly like a ballerina, had a look of secret detachment: Eve recognised her from the photograph on her husband's desk. Laura Stevens greeted her prettily. One had to learn, Eve thought, that to these people she was a woman alone, and that long and clamorous life with Jamie, which was so vivid in her own head, did not exist for them. She must not, of course, continue to talk about it, for people wanted to discuss the present, not the past.

At dinner she found herself between Rufus Stevens and Giles

Ransome. Light was going out of the day, and the table was lit with candles. Yet the curtains were not drawn, and through the french windows she could see the vanishing image of the garden, late roses losing colour, and trace the fading line of hills. The contrast of lights seemed to suggest mystery, and for a time she lost the voices of those about the table and entered a place of unknown dimensions, even balm. Perhaps grief was a necessary, transient thing, such as the passing from light to dark, to light again. Perhaps this not quite earthly colour of air, with ghosts of the candle flames painted in the darkening windows, suggested that nothing was as it seemed; that death and pain had no final significance; that one step from this seemingly solid world could take her to a place of unimagined ease. Perhaps all occasions invited His mercies, and all times were His seasons . . .

Rufus Stevens' voice recalled her to the present. '. . . of course, we're all concerned with the future of our children. What the hell are they going to do? Mark's not interested in business——'

Lynton draped one arm over the back of his chair. 'Oh — *business*. With due respect, how can anyone be *interested* in business? It's something that has to happen, like sewage and bad weather.'

Rufus Stevens faced Lynton with the controlled antagonism of a man used to dealing with opponents on whom he has no intention of spending too much energy. 'As you so rightly say — business is as necessary as sewage and bad weather, both of which we have always with us. Personally I don't find it boring, because I've succeeded at it and nothing you succeed at is boring: that's one of the not surprising rules. Laura finds it boring, of course, but then wives do.' Laura made a face to show that she did indeed find it boring; and Rufus went on, 'Though she does — I hope — enjoy the fruits of it.'

Henry Boyle flushed and said, 'I think that's rather unfair.'

Rufus turned on him the same look that he had given Lynton. 'Do you? I don't think statements of fact can be unfair. I don't blame Laura for liking the swimming-pool and being bored by what makes it possible for her to have one.'

Laura said with a laugh which didn't quite ring true, 'Rufus always manages to make me sound very silly. I'm sure he doesn't mean it, but that's how I feel.'

Henry muttered something inaudible. Julia Ransome passed a hand over her smooth dark hair and said, 'Oh, *all* our husbands make us feel foolish from time to time.'

82

Giles Ransome said, 'My dear — there's no question of making you feel foolish. Headmasters get swamped by their job, I'm afraid, and are notorious for talking shop.' He moved the silver candlestick in front of him a fraction to the left. 'Julia does her best as a headmaster's wife, but she finds it hard. I don't blame her: schoolboys are an acquired taste, and I must say I haven't in all cases acquired it myself. Julia isn't a committee woman, and the sight of a pack of sweaty boys in running shorts gives her no sort of pleasure — one isn't really surprised.'

Julia said, 'That may be, but I married a schoolmaster.'

'Possibly to your regret.' The words were spoken lightly, but Julia didn't deny them.

Laura Stevens cried, with the shrill anxiety of a hostess aware of contrary winds, 'Oh, I think it's so important to be able to tease your partner: that's the important thing, when it doesn't *matter* what one says to the other.'

'Oh . . . it matters.' Julia turned her dark glance towards her. 'Some of the sharpest weapons find their mark within the so-called pleasantries of marriage — wouldn't you agree?' She addressed Rufus, who lifted his brows and said, 'That could be — could be.'

'All this is much too clever for me,' Laura said. '*I* don't use any weapons — do I, Henry?'

Henry cleared his throat and said No, she didn't.

Rufus pushed at his glass. 'I suppose there is more than one kind of weapon——'

Eve put her face briefly in her hands, then looked up, trusting that the movement had gone unnoticed. For it was of course absurd to scream silently within herself, *Don't* quarrel, don't argue: you are both alive. The asymmetry of grief gave to one's imagination too great a simplicity, perhaps sentiment. Marriage became blessed in whatever form; the words 'our' and 'we' had bloom on them. Of course she and Jamie had sometimes fought; but these moments had no power now except to wound. Perhaps she should look on them in some other way? For after all to believe that marriage had been perfect was to diminish it, to make it unreal, and one could not mourn an unreality.

'Just think,' Laura was saying with the continued desperation of an unnerved hostess, 'Mark and Nigel are already in *Spain*——'

'Andorra,' her husband corrected her, 'is a principality——'

'Oh, Rufus, darling, I don't know anything about politics or principalities.'

'I'm just trying to point out that Andorra isn't Spain; it's independent.'

'But they talk Spanish, don't they?'

'Catalan,' Giles Ransome said. 'And they're very proud of being Andorrans, having survived, since the time of Charlemagne, from the assaults of the Moors ... No, I'm not going to give a lecture, my dear,' he said to his wife, 'so don't look as if you thought I were.'

'Well, Spain or Andorra, Nigel and Mark are there,' Laura said, still high-pitched. 'Learning to live out of doors. Terribly good for them, I expect, though Mark'll hate it if it rains.'

'Then he'll hate it,' Eve said, momentarily diverted by this view of the expedition, 'for at some time or other in the mountains, it always rains.'

Later, Rufus, smoking a cigar, walked with Eve in the garden. Warmth from the day lingered, and though it was dark, the late roses still bloomed, white as moths, and the scent of grass rose strongly, with some essence that was different from the day. From the room they had left, light and sound of voices carried faintly into the dusk.

Rufus said, 'Perhaps we were an ill-assorted party. But one can never be sure when the wires will cross.'

'It wasn't important.'

'I think perhaps it was, to you.'

She was again surprised by his perception; the sense of greeting a friend when lost in strange country. Reminded of the encounter with Jamie's father, she thought that this bleak time had its mercy, for she could not imagine that if Jamie had been alive she would have made either of these discoveries.

The garden was long and now the lighted window seemed far off. They trod dark unseen grass, and a night wind turned the leaves, and sent the cigar smoke astream. The swimming-pool wore a black snake-like skin, and the white chairs ranged about it were dull, like bones.

She said, 'Your wife isn't at all worried about the expedition, is she?'

'Laura doesn't know much about mountains, and she hasn't a very strong imagination. However, I'm sure she's correct to make light of it.'

Cigar scent, the blanched cool roses, the deepening dark. She strolled, silent, beside Rufus, till she became aware of other voices in the garden. Some distance away, hushed, smothered laughter, but unmistakable: Laura Stevens and Henry Boyle. 'We can't stay here — I have to go back — I'm the hostess. Besides, I don't know where Rufus is.' 'Never mind. Just for a moment — anyone can be lost for a moment.' The smothered, ruffled sounds of an embrace. 'We must go back——' 'No, please——' 'Yes, I must . . . later, perhaps.'

At Eve's side, Rufus was now unmoving, except to draw on his cigar: she saw the end glow. She could think of nothing that would fit the sting and embarrassment of the moment. At last he said, 'It will be best to let them go back. Showdowns, especially in front of guests, aren't in my line.'

Slowly he turned and began to walk back to the house. After a few moments he said, 'You mustn't think too badly of Laura. She's very pretty, and she finds me dull.' She could see in the dusk that he had braced his shoulders. 'Of course I may be to her, but I'm not the *worst* kind of bore. I know all about bores: they come in different degrees, and the worst are the ones that can't listen — ever.' He touched her arm, not with surreptitious contact, but with affection. 'Rough roads, sometimes,' he said. 'However, you need, I'm sure, have no fears about Nigel. Lightning doesn't strike twice. Is that a crude way to put it? Well, I'm a crude man.'

'No, I don't think so.'

'Oh, you mustn't believe that because I can talk to an attractive widow in a dark garden I have any particular merit, or indeed finesse.'

She shook her head. Rufus Stevens knew the landscape of dark country.

But as they returned to the lighted room, where those within it had the blank startled look of people caught by a flash photographer, she became aware that this day was nearly gone: one more and she would be on her way home, back to the silence again, this fragile contact of sympathy broken, perhaps for ever.

While Rufus offered night-caps to the company, without meeting the eyes of his wife and Henry Boyle, the knot formed in her chest: this room was a transient place, and its voices and conflicts would cease. She saw her hand shiver as Rufus handed her a glass, and he said, 'Was it cold in the garden?'

'No.' They spoke under the other voices which were alive again.

'I was thinking about going home.'

He nodded, as if he understood. He paid no attention to his wife and Henry Boyle who both had now a look of faint discomfiture. He said, 'Don't expect to find a postcard from Nigel. Postcards from places like Andorra lie in some especial foreign cave for about three weeks before anyone attempts to send them on.'

'Yes, I know.' But of course she would think about Nigel when she was back in town, in the silence. Waiting. Absurd, for there was nothing to wait for, except his return, which would not be long delayed.

7

The morning trailed mists over the high peaks. The mists were cold, having within them the taste of snow. Already, wearing an orange anorak, Larry Howard was striding between the tents; 'Come along! Nice running water not far away to wash in . . . time to get up; no one's going to bring you a cup of tea.'

Nigel turned in his sleeping-bag. His body ached from the hard ground, and though the tent had a furry warmth from the bodies and breath of other boys, cold slid a hand between his shoulder-blades. Mark opened his eyes. 'Oh God, we're still here. I was dreaming I was back home, asleep beside the swimming-pool. Can't anyone stop Howard from being so damn jolly?'

Nigel worked himself out of his sleeping bag. Cold enveloped him. Taking a towel he said, 'Coming to wash?'

Mark turned over. 'Oh, God, *wash*. Masochism. I thought this was going to be a splendid time in the sun. I've only seen the sun for about ten minutes.'

'The mountains are lovely,' Nigel said.

'When you can see them.'

'Aren't you enjoying it?' Nigel asked, while Crawley (Philip) and Fenstone (Kenneth) reluctantly pulled themselves from their sleeping-bags.

'Hard to say.' Mark himself had made no effort to move or to respond to Howard's calls. 'It's all so enormously different from what I'd imagined. *Andorra*. Anything ending in "a" like that ought to be soaked in sun. This . . . it's more like the scenery for some ghastly Wagnerian opera I was taken to once — how I hate opera,' he added.

Another roar from Howard.

'I thought this was meant to be a holiday,' Mark said; 'More like a concentration camp . . . All right, I'm coming.'

Shivering, Nigel led the small company of boys to the fish-silver river which ran fast over flat grey stones. Gene Carson, less voluble than Howard (and less strident, in dark blue) wandered with them. 'That's the Arinsal,' he said. 'It comes from high up there,

87

near to the Spanish border . . . Yeah, I know it's cold, but you'll get over it. And down there, several thousand feet below, it joins the Valira del Nord. Some guy, I forget who, said that the sound of running water was "the eternal anthem of the valley". Guess that was before the tourists brought their Volkswagons, but you might say it was true.'

Though their waters were snow-cold, Nigel liked the rivers, galloping fast over cold stones. He liked too the high and lonely peaks, so much taller and more forbidding than the Cumbrian hills he knew. Sometimes he stood tranced by the steep lift of rock which cut the air with the incision of a curved blade, and the lonely places where the snow still lingered like an icy fleece.

But when he tried to convey this to Mark, he felt the blank of a piano note which gives no sound. Mark was not enjoying the mountains, or the icy streams or the climbing instruction. He wanted to wander off with Nigel and find a taverna and drink coffee and talk.

'But you knew it was an outdoor thing,' Nigel said.

'I didn't know outdoors was going to be so bloody cold.'

'If you put sweaters on and climb, you get hot.'

'I don't; I'm cold all the time.'

'You can't be; when we walked down to Pal yesterday——'

'And that's another thing. How can a village be called Pal? Honestly. I thought foreign names were marvellous and exotic, like Andalucia, Malaga, Sorrento. *Pal.*'

'But it's a lovely place,' Nigel said, disconsolate.

'Don't look so solemn. Yes, if it weren't for you, I'd rather be at home, or practically anywhere. But you *are* here, so I'll take Howard's obscene jocularity, all this over-kill of fresh air, just for that.'

Comfort of a kind; but he said, 'I thought we liked the same things.'

'Oh, Lord. Well, we do. No one likes *everything* the same. You were taken climbing as a tot, it's in your blood. I don't think Pa or Ma have got nearer to climbing a mountain than using the staircase when a lift's out of order.'

Nigel reflected on Mark's parents: no, neither of them would have much time for mountains.

But he — yes, he loved them. He hadn't known how much till now. Perhaps, when he had climbed with his father he had been overwhelmed by his father's prowess and fame; perhaps by a fear that he might fail. But now these heights were his own.

He came out of a dream where he surmounted some untrodden summit, to hear Howard say, 'We're going to take the jeeps down to Andorra La Vella; then to Encamp——'

Mark said to Nigel: '*Told* you! How can one have a village called Encamp? It sounds like Butlins.'

'From Encamp we take the cable car which climbs a few thousand feet up to the Lake of Engolasters——'

'Now I've heard everything,' Mark said.

As the jeep, driven by Gene Carson, took the great sweeps of the road downwards, Nigel felt a double thrust of disappointment: he didn't want to go down to the noisy town of Andorra La Vella, and he didn't like this division from Mark. He tried to take comfort from the drive, when a village was first a thousand feet below, then all about them; white modern buildings strident amongst the old grey limestone houses with wooden balconies and the tobacco leaves like brown aprons hung out to dry. As they drove, the mist dissolved, drifting like smoke below them, and light from an emerging sun infused the smoke with colour.

By the time they reached Andorra La Vella the sun clear of mist beat strongly, intensifying the noisy traffic, the crowds on the narrow pavements, the harsh music from the souvenir shops, and the supermarkets which had piled outside on the pavements stacks of whisky, brandy and gin. Mark, taking out some tattered peseta notes with authority said, 'Promised the parents I'd bring some of this stuff back.'

Nigel waited in the sunlit street, the harsh Catalan language about him. What was wrong with this day? True, he didn't like the town, even though the heights loomed above it, and the sun was hot with a southern strength . . .

He said as Mark joined him, weighted with a plastic bag, 'I'll be glad to get out of here.'

Mark looked up the jangling street. 'Honestly? I think it's rather fun. Better than that gruesome cold water and bare rock.'

Still shadowed by disappointment, Nigel walked beside him to the jeep. 'Can't help thinking,' he said, looking back to the crowded commerce of the street, 'how Ma got it wrong — she saw me balanced on a rock face, and here we are, practically in Woolworths.'

'Not for long. We're set for the cable car.'

'That'll be fun.'

Mark didn't at once reply. 'Yes, I suppose so. What kind are they? The sort where your legs hang out?'

'No, I don't think so. I saw a picture: they looked like closed-in side-cars.'

Fine weather still held as the jeep bounded and swept away from the town. Well, that's better, Nigel thought. Mark beside him was unexpectedly silent. Gene Carson said above the noisy engine, 'The road goes on beyond Encamp to Meritxell which is a shrine with a famous Virgin — don't snigger, Crawley: you know what I mean: she's the patron saint of Andorra. Then on to Canillo and Soldeu. I've ski-ed in Soldeu. *Not* too well organised: the chair-lift stuck, and we were high and dry for what seemed hours, but it was fun.'

'Stuck?' Mark said, but Gene made no reply; perhaps he didn't hear. As they drove into Encamp, Nigel could already see the white pylons of the cable-cars, and the small coloured cabins — blue, yellow and red — as they climbed slowly, one side upwards and the other down, above the tall firs on the mountain side. Mark was still silent.

The small cabins held two people, sitting face to face, knees almost touching. The boys, with Carson and Howard, queued up in a shed, where a man in shirt sleeves, sweating from the heat, slammed the door of the cabin, pulled a chain which sent the small craft inexorably on and upward.

The shed was dark, cut off from the sun, and smelt of sweat and machinery. They watched as the pairs ahead of them were slammed and sealed into the cabins, and sent on their way. 'It's a bit like an execution shed, isn't it?' Mark said, speaking after a long silence.

'Never seen one,' Nigel replied.

It was their turn. Nigel climbed in first. The small cabin, despite its glowing colour, was dingy and even smelly inside. Mark put himself on the seat facing upward; the door was slammed, a key turned. Nigel laughed and said, 'Now we can't get out, no way.'

The man pulled a chain ('Remind you of anything?' Nigel said); and the small smelly cabin swung out of the shed and upward.

Nigel felt a shift of excitement. The little cabin drifted slowly higher, leaving the shed behind; yet in spite of its slowness seemed quickly to gain height. The tall tops of the fir trees were below their feet and the wide air about them. As the cabin climbed towards the first pylon it slowed, swayed, made a rattling noise and appeared to lose heart. Nigel, who had been looking up over

90

his shoulder, turned back and said, 'All change for Clapham Junction.'

Mark had his head between his knees.

Nigel said, 'What's up?'

The cabin, having negotiated the pylon, was gaining equilibrium and its original speed. Mark lifted his head; his face had lost colour, his forehead was wet. He said, 'I thought we were going to go backwards, or get stuck like Carson.'

'They always make you feel like that.'

'Been on one before?'

'Yes.'

Mark nodded, his eyes down, not looking at the long high distance to the next pylon, nor to the growing skiey depth below them, but at the shabby floor at his feet.

Nigel sat in the small swaying cabin, puzzled, even disturbed. Always, Mark had been the leader, the one whose affection he feared to lose. There was nothing, Nigel had supposed, that he could do better than Mark. Yet now, while Nigel was engrossed and excited, Mark was obviously scared stiff. So scared that he couldn't look out of the window or indeed anywhere but at his feet.

Nigel frowned. Strange. His impulse should surely be to give reassurance, but his main feeling was one of surprise, mixed with a cold thread of contempt. This shocked him; he sat some thousand feet and more in the air, and took the effect of the shock.

It brought first before him an unforeseen picture: of his mother alone in the flat, of the pages on the writing desk. And he felt more strongly that there was something wrong with this day . . .

The cabin swayed on, while on the parallel wire other cabins slid downwards to the shed, which now looked very small: a toy structure, bright in the valley sun. Another pylon; the cabin swinging at the airy height. Nigel kept his eyes on Mark. Though he wanted to look away, he found he could not. Mark was very frightened, and Nigel had no means of easing him.

Nigel said, 'Only four more to go.'

Mark nodded. 'All right. But — hell — we've got to go *back*.' He gave a quick look at the cabins passing downward.

'Not so bad,' Nigel said. 'You get nearer the ground. Like flying, and coming to land. But you didn't mind that.'

'It was different. Something to do with being *not* connected to the earth.'

They reached the top; sprang out into the shed, and then into the warm sun. They could still see the cable cars moving slowly, small now, like child's toys on a wire. When Howard had counted the company once more, they wandered through a pine-shaded path, to the Lake of Engolasters. (The words meant 'Swallower of Stars' Carson said; because in summer the shooting stars seemed to drown in its waters.) Now its calm water was painted blue by the sky. As they sat, surrounded by boulders and scrubby grass, Nigel said, 'It might be anywhere: the Lakes or Wales or Scotland.'

'This is all right,' Mark allowed; 'blue water is always agreeable.'

His usual tone of light mockery had returned, but it didn't quite ring true, and Nigel thought the wind of estrangement blew between them.

This seemed to strengthen as they came to the ancient church of San Miguel. The church with its tall tower stood alone, as if it grew from the rocks. 'Used to be a village here,' Carson said, 'nothing of it remains. Only the empty church among the mountain peaks. Ghosts may hang around, but the people are gone.'

Mark said under his breath, 'Not surprised; I'd be gone too.'

Pointing to the mountain heads across the valley, Carson said, 'There are the passes into France and Spain — men fled over them one way in the Civil War (1936: history to you, I suppose); and the other way in the *last* war, when Spain was neutral, and the Allies came through the network of the Resistance to make their way to Lisbon. Some never made it — the Pyrenees in winter can kill as well as any sniper or machine-gun.

Nigel looked up at the tall heads, some still veined with snow. In imagination he could see a great army of ragged soldiers, frozen, wounded, some finding at last the safety of the valley.

'It must have been exciting,' he said to Mark.

'*Exciting* — it must've been hell. If I'd been a prisoner, I'd've stayed where I was.'

He spoke with force: clearly the betrayal of fear still shadowed him: he was ashamed of it, and angry that he was ashamed. By the time they reached the lonely tower of the church of San Miguel, Mark was under a sullen cloud of resentment. When Nigel went into the confines of the church with the others, Mark stayed outside. 'Churches bore me,' he said. 'All churches bore me: I don't mind if they were built before the Flood; I still don't want to see them.' When Nigel came into the sun again, Mark was wandering back to the lake. Nigel said, 'There wasn't much to see: it was too dark. It looks better from outside.'

'Churches usually do.'

'I like the tower.' Nigel looked back. 'It's so high, and out of proportion. I like things to be out of proportion; not made to a pattern.'

'That sounds a bit classy to me. Like something you read.'

Nigel, after one look of surprise, said, 'Well, maybe it was. I don't remember. It's true, anyway. Perhaps that's why I like mountains and don't like rows of houses.'

'Very philosophical.'

'I don't know why you're being so sarcastic about everything.'

'I'm not being sarcastic. I just find churches boring, and I think it's boring when you go on about the tower being too high for the rest of it. Who cares?'

Nigel was silent. He seldom quarrelled with Mark, and the rare experience, intensified by the beauty about them, and the distance from home, shadowed the day. And it was no good arguing with Mark about the tower of San Miguel, because that had in truth nothing to do with the matter.

So they walked in charged and unhappy silence (while Larry Howard counted everyone again, and Gene Carson talked easily to those near him) back towards the *telecabines*.

'. . . Any of you know why the Pyrenees are so called?' Gene was saying. 'There's a legend that Hercules, when drunk, ravished a young girl — again, there's no need to snigger, Crawley, and yes, you *do* know what ravished means — and the girl's name was Pyrène, and she died of grief. (Yes, Fenstone; at being ravished — those were other times.) When he'd sobered up, Hercules in the toils of remorse went about these parts making the whole range echo with her name. In case any of you get carried away by this story, I should add that Pliny considered it to be idle fiction.'

Nigel glanced at Mark to see if he was amused at Gene Carson's dry postscript, but his head was down, and he said nothing. As they got into the coloured cabin, Nigel saw that Mark's hand shook. The air of antagonism prevailed, within the confined space, on the journey down.

It prevailed through the next lap of their journey, to the Col de la Botella, one of the passes into Spain. 'Don't try wandering off,' Gene said, 'because the Pyrenees stretch for a hundred and twenty-five miles, and have a breadth of sixty. And one summit looks very much the same as another.'

Out of the jeep, Nigel stood beside Gene and looked down the rough slopes, into Spain. Sore from the quarrel, longing to get closer to this country which was so much to his liking, Nigel said to him, 'When do we do some climbing?'

'Tomorrow, if the weather holds.'

'Does it matter about the weather?'

'You bet your sweet life it does. If you've not seen a Pyrenean storm, you've seen nothing yet. Take a wrong path in the mists, lose your way, and . . . well, I suppose the next thing would be your frozen body as meat for the wolves or bears——'

'*Are* there bears?' asked Fenstone (Kenneth), more interested in this than Nigel's frozen body.

'There used to be. I daresay the tourists have driven them out.'

Mark was still silent. Nigel moved away from him, away from the mixture of sorrow and anger. As he climbed the rough ground, he saw a small stone shed. It seemed, like the church of San Miguel, to grow out of the rocks —

'*Buenos diás!*'

He stopped, startled. A man came from the side of the hut. He wore muddy blue corduroy trousers, a kind of battered jockey cap, and was repairing the wall of the stone cabin with cement and a trowel.

Nigel said, 'Hullo. D'you speak English?'

The man smiled, showing large yellowish teeth. His eyes were friendly, but he shook his head. '*Un poquito . . .*'

Nigel looked into the cabin. The inside had an air of comfort: there was a wooden bunk, covered with straw; a wine bottle; wood laid for a fire (he'd noticed a small chimney in the slate roof); food on a shelf. The air was close, but not ill-smelling.

Nigel, by means of words and gestures, asked the man if he slept there. The man nodded and glanced at the sun. '*En el verano . . .*' Yes, Nigel said; he understood: in summer the man slept there. But now? Tonight?

The man shook his head. '*En el invierno . . . Anyos.*' He made the gesture of one who clasps himself against cold, and pointed with his thumb to a village in the steep depths of the valley.

'But it's not winter yet,' Nigel protested.

Possibly the words were understood. He grinned, and looked up at the sky where the sun blazed. '*Tempestad,*' he said.

Nigel lifted his head, puzzled. A breeze, perhaps, at this height, and cloud like a small stain on a far peak; but elsewhere the rocky ground gave back the sun.

'*Tempestad*?' He made a guess. 'Storm?'

'*Si . . . pronto . . . El buen tiempo terminará.*' He waved a hand at the sun, as if he dispensed with it.

Nigel nodded, not quite believing him, because countrymen the world over, he imagined, liked to show wisdom about the weather. 'Are you a shepherd?' he asked.

The man seemed to understand better than he spoke. He shook his head, and pointed to the silk-brown cattle which grazed on the greener grass below him.

'Oh, a cow-herd,' Nigel said. He thought he wouldn't mind being a cow-herd, living in the summer months at this height, with food and drink and the lonely hills . . . And at once he knew how little Mark would like to be a cow-herd.

Nigel turned away, and the man lifted a hand with the trowel. '*Adios!*'

Nigel called back, '*Adios!*' running over the stony ground.

Returned to the camp they ate in the still warm air, by the stream. Comforted by the food, and the magnificence about them, Nigel said as if Mark were his accustomed self, 'We're climbing tomorrow.'

Mark looked up. 'Where?'

'Golly, where d'you think? Shepherd's Bush? *Here*. Must be climbs all over the place.'

Mark looked up to the tall enclosing peaks. 'I've never done any climbing.'

'Simple enough on the rope. You can't fall off; just dangle for a few minutes in space.'

The words were spoken lightly; Nigel was surprised when Mark said with anger, 'Don't be so bloody superior.'

'I'm not.'

'Yes, you are.' (They sounded like children, Nigel thought.) 'Just because I didn't like the cable car, you want to get at me about climbing——'

'I don't want to get at you about anything,' The ease of food and warmth had gone. Angry too he said, 'I wanted to have fun. I thought that was why we came. You said it was. That's why I came, when my mother——'

'Oh Lord, your mother. She wanted to bitch the whole thing:

yes, I know that.'

Nigel dug his boot into the rocky earth. 'All right, she had a thing about it. I know it seemed a bit much, but my father——'

'There wasn't any need to make such a fuss. Lots of mothers have sons who go all over the place. An outing like this, with old Howard and Gene keeping us in like sheepdogs——'

'There's a bit in the small print which says the school can't be responsible——'

'Lord, that was just routine——'

'It was there. She read it.'

'I don't get you at all. I honestly don't. You were mad keen to come on this do; you were in a frightful bate when your mother made all that fuss, and now you're taking her side——'

'I'm not taking anyone's side. I'm just saying I understand why she went into a spin about it all.'

'Golly, you really have got a lot to learn——'

'What the hell d'you mean?'

'Mothers are O.K., but you have to get free of them. They try to smother you. Ever so nicely, of course, but it's a massive operation. And you're falling for it.'

'I'm not! I came, didn't I?'

'And now you wish you hadn't?'

(Perhaps this was true.) 'No ... but I keep thinking about her——'

'I *told* you. Get out from under. All right, she lost your father: I'm sorry, but lots of women get to be widows. They have the guts to go on alone——'

'She has got guts!'

'O.K.; calm down; what the hell does it matter? I don't think she has, as a matter of fact——'

'You're a bloody liar.'

'Lord ... Lord. A mother fixation, and we never knew——'

'I haven't. I'm not.' Nigel found himself near to tears with rage and lost love. 'And if you knew what I did about your mother——'

'What the hell d'you mean?'

'I saw her,' Nigel said, reckless with anger. 'I saw her that time I came to stay, when Lynton and Henry Boyle were there.'

'What d'you mean, you saw her?'

Nigel swallowed, for a moment wishing to draw back. Too late now. 'I came into the house when you were all out——'

'Well?'

'I saw your mother and Henry Boyle——' he stopped, now ashamed.

'Snogging, you mean? Why not, and what the hell's it to do with you?'

'Nothing, I daresay.'

'Precisely. She's grown-up and her life's her own.' More bravado in his voice than conviction, perhaps. 'If you believed you could get back at me on that one — sorry, chum, but you missed out.'

'You said my mother hadn't got guts. That's a pretty rotten thing to say.'

Mark shrugged. 'You can't deny, she made one hell of a fuss.'

'Oh, bloody *leave* it. You don't understand. You don't understand one bit.'

'Moronic now, I suppose.'

'You're a different person from what I thought.'

'Oh, come of it. You're talking like some tiresome girl. All this carry on because I don't much care for the outdoor life.'

'It isn't only that . . .'

'I told you — you've got to get clear of your Ma. Whether she's in trouble or not.'

'I *am*——'

'No, you're not. You were all right till we started to argue, and then it's all a kind of run back to Mum.'

'It isn't. It isn't. I've told you, I saw her, how she was. It was a big thing. You weren't there. You don't know. No one who wasn't there can know.'

'Oh, we're on to that now, are we: high up the ladder; the chap who's seen it all——'

'And as for guts,' Nigel went on, stung and reckless, 'what sort of guts did you show in the cable car?'

'You are a little *creep*, aren't you?' Mark said, white now and angry. 'All right, I didn't like it, and what the hell. Only an absolute *creep* would bring it up.'

Nigel was silent. His heart was going fast, and a little thrum of blood beat in his head. Sorrow gripped his chest, for this journey had been desired above all else: blotting out the memory of the lakeland grave, and his mother afterwards; and those pages of 'confession' read at night . . .

But something had gone wrong with the adventure, badly

wrong, and now he remembered his walk alone at Rosthwaite, back to the grave, in the diminishing light, with the hills darkening about him ... Other hills than these, the hills of home, far from where he sat now, angry and estranged from Mark, whom he had loved. (Somewhere he had read that there were two tragedies in life: one was *not* to get what you wanted, and the other was to get it. He'd wanted to come here, but ...)

About their silence came the voices of the other boys, of Howard's cheerful arguments, and Gene's comfortable drawl. Their own small and angry silence endured, as the sun slipped below the level of the high mountain heads, and the dark and the cold crept upon them like marauders.

'Climbing tomorrow,' Howard said, shifting coils of rope, as they returned to their tents. 'Mind you put on your boots, warm sweaters, everything you've got. We could try a little way up the Pic Pedrosa there. A day's trip, so fill your rucksacks with all you can. And brew up something hot for your Thermos. If anyone gets stuck, that could be all-important.'

Gene said, 'What about the weather? Cloud over there.'

Howard shook his head. 'Set fair, I should say.'

'Bit of a wind getting up.'

'It always does at evening.'

'Maybe. But it's late in the season. Our luck must change soon.'

'Not yet.'

Once in the tent and within the grateful warmth of his sleeping-bag, Nigel lay long awake. The rest of them, he thought, including Mark, were asleep. Crawley (Philip) snored gently. Mark had not spoken again; between them lay a sword of silence. The words of the quarrel repeated themselves with the persistence of a recording in Nigel's head, producing a cold heaviness within him, as if he'd eaten something ill-digested. Round and round; the climb in the cable car, the sight of Mark's fear ... Was that where it had begun? Perhaps earlier; perhaps there had been something wrong from the beginning, from the moment they had set out from Perpignan. Perhaps even before that.

He could hear the sound of the river running fast over the stones, as if a company of people went with hushed and multiplied voices in the dark, and the cry of the wind as it drove through the narrow passes between the rocks. At last, to the accompaniment of these sounds which carried menace within them, he slept.

§

He woke of a sudden, severed from some uncomfortable dream.

Larry Howard was standing over him, his hand on Nigel's shoulder. 'Come on, Rutherford: where d'you think you are? Day for the climb: everyone's ahead of you.'

Head aching, clumsy with surprise and lack of sleep, Nigel saw that the others were dressed and preparing breakfast. He pulled on his clothes awkwardly, went to the makeshift latrine within its canvas cover, returned to wash briefly in the cold running river — the river which he seemed to have heard all night. Even the icy water didn't revive him: he stumbled as he walked back to the camp, and wiped his forehead which seemed cold and sweaty at the same time. He tried to remember his dream, but though it had disturbed him, there remained only the disturbance, an echo of loud voices whose words he couldn't recall.

As he drank from the mug of cocoa and ate the rye bread, the sour taste of the day before returned. Mark still paid him no attention. Nigel thought, *He might have woken me*; but tried to dismiss the thought: clear that the feud still held.

He returned quickly to the tent. What had Howard said yesterday? Sweaters ... food ... The tent was empty, and his scrambling efforts to prepare himself for the day had the confused hurry of one who tries to catch a train against time.

When he came out of the tent he found Gene Carson and Howard talking together, their voices raised in argument.

'No harm in setting out,' Howard was saying; 'A little cloud over there to the east, but otherwise, the sky's clear: looks like yesterday. *If* it turns nasty — which I doubt — we can come back.'

Carson said, 'Uh-huh,' hands in his pockets, lifting his head as if to smell the weather. 'I'm not for it,' he said. 'I think we should wait to see what happens. I know these parts——'

'So do I——'

'Storms come with astonishing suddenness. Rain like a wall, mist, cold. The cold's the worst, and the most dangerous.'

'I'm not leading them into any danger——'

Nigel listened with impatience, half-held within the unformed images of his dream. He wanted to go on the climb: it had purpose, it would be an escape from the shadow of yesterday. He looked towards Mark, but he was apparently lost in conversation.

Howard said, 'Well, that's it then. We agree to differ.'

'Seems so,' said Gene.

'You'll allow that I'm the senior in this outfit?'

'Oh, sure.'

'Then I shall take a party — voluntary, of course — of those boys who want to come. What you'll do——'

'Take them fishing, perhaps. Good in rainy weather.'

'Don't think it's going to rain. However, we've been into that. Hands up, those who want to come with me.'

Nigel put up his hand at once, without thought. Mark's hands stayed in his pockets, his head down. Of course he isn't coming, Nigel thought; but sadness rather than contempt held him now. Who *was* coming? In the event only four of the rest of the company. Dimly, Nigel felt surprise.

He pulled on his rucksack, still with the sense that this day was out of focus, and glanced at his companions. Crawley (Philip) his dark hair spiky from his morning wash; Fenstone (Kenneth), his glasses shining in the early sun, looking up to the slopes with calculation, as if he were solving a mathematical problem (maths was his subject, Nigel recalled); Vernon (Gerald) was a good rugger and cricket player, but short on academic prowess: Nigel could see him in Latin lessons, baffled as a dog whose cat-quarry has just climbed a tree. Merryweather (Frederick) was the son of a playwright whose work appeared on television, giving him a gleam of reflected glory. A talkative boy with odd angular movements; he wrote with nervous speed, in a handwriting which appeared to be going headlong off the page. Mark had said of him once, 'I believe he's training to be a genius.'

So these were they, the four of them; five with Nigel; six with Larry Howard.

'All ready?' Howard was saying. 'Fine. Remember everything I've told you. I'll be in the lead. We shan't need the rope at first: as you see, the slopes are easy enough to begin with.' He turned to Gene — 'O.K. — you know where we're going. What do the Spanish say? *Adios*, I believe. We'll be back before dark.'

As the small party turned to begin the climb, Nigel looked back, prepared to lift a hand in farewell to Mark, but Mark had turned away.

This small last cut drove Nigel to walk quickly, head down, up the first rough path. All he wanted was to get amongst these hills, away from contention, away from Mark who had been the golden aspect of life, and seemed to be so no more.

Within this anger, he heard Howard's voice: 'Hey! You — Rutherford! Who the hell d'you think's leading this party? *I* am . Don't go so fast.'

Nigel waited while Howard came panting up beside him. 'Got to remember your orders, old chap. Can't play about with these mountains, as I said. I did say that, didn't I? *I'm* leading this, and I don't want any stupid rebel outbreaks from any of you. Gene — Mr Carson and I disagree about this climb; well, I'm going to prove him wrong — get that?'

Yes, Nigel thought: he got it. Howard's pride was at stake: the latent antagonism between the two of them had strengthened. The safety of his party was important, of course, but so also was the need to prove himself right and Carson wrong.

Nigel let Howard and the other boys go ahead of him, as he went more slowly. After a while he stood to stare at the heights above him; the bare rocks began to ease the rub of anger and poor sleep . . .

'*Rutherford!* What the hell d'you think you're doing now? I said let me lead: I didn't say turn into a pillar of salt and look at the sky.' Howard, as he easily could, was losing his temper.

Silent, Nigel moved on. Everyone knew about Howard: he had to have someone to be angry with, and on this expedition it was going to be him. Well, he'd asked for it; he must try not to ask for it again.

They climbed on. The wind freshened; the square new houses of a village, some thousand feet below, were transformed with light. As the company drew higher, he was glad to leave the valley behind, to leave Mark behind. Did some ghost accompany him? He was more aware of his father than of the boys and Howard who climbed with him. His head still ached, and the stony path at his feet seemed at moments to swim and fade.

The climb grew steeper. He paused to get his breath. Had the sun gone in? Certainly the wind was rising, and all the valley below them dark, the white houses gleaming no more.

Head down, he turned to climb on.

At first he barely noticed the mist. It seemed only a softening of outline, of tree and stone, a quietening of the sound of water. He trudged on. Then suddenly as if by some transforming magic, the mist was all about him, rolling like huge breakers, forming and re-forming, but allowing him to see nothing more than itself, not even the shape of a rock; barely the path at his feet.

He stood still and listened. Howard and the rest must be ahead of him: he remembered Howard's call to get behind and let him lead. Indeed, it seemed to him that he could hear their voices, but they were muffled, as was all sound, by the mist. They must be far ahead; he'd been lost in his dreams and lingered behind.

He began to go more quickly. The mist was cold, seeming to force itself down his throat and into his chest. Baffling, total, silent, except for the far moaning of the wind. Faster, then; to catch up with them, to be one of a company, for the vast whiteness about him, and the great unseen towers of the Pyrenees touched the nerve of warning. Faster, stumbling because of the mist, and because of the cloud in his head, the almost sleepless night. Faster, to reach the voices ... He paused, gasping from speed, from the mist in his throat, from the first of fear.

For now he could not hear the voices. He stood still, rubbing his ear, as if the fog had muffled it. They must have gone further ahead than he knew; he had, of course, only to spur himself and he would find them, for they must be on the same path, and Larry Howard's bulk in its orange anorak would loom clear before him, and fear would be done.

He climbed the rough track as fast as he could, until he heard the sound of his breath, loud, like the sea in his ears. He paused again and tried to listen, above the sound of his own breathing. The mist kept rolling towards him in enveloping clouds. For brief moments it broke, but only to show some snatched glimpse of far mountainside, then the white penetrating silence surrounded him again.

Nothing but silence, and the distant wind, like something imprisoned within the heights. No voices, not even the echo of Howard's voice, calling for him. He shivered, for the mist was cold, as if it carried ice at its heart. He tried to think. After all, he knew about mountain mists; with his father he had met them often enough in the hills. Clear before his mind's eye he could see his father, tall, bearded, beside him in a mist, taking out his compass ...

A compass. He hadn't got a compass. No one — had they? — had said anything about a compass. He supposed Howard had one, but what use was that to him, Nigel, here apart from the rest? He felt a sting of rage, the rage of exhaustion and fear. He tried to swallow it down, because he knew it would do him no good.

He had to think. If perhaps he waited here, on the path, Howard would return and find him. Howard wouldn't surely climb on in the mist, even though retreat would prove that Gene had been right about the day. Soon Howard must reappear; he had only to wait. Perhaps the mist might dissolve, and clarity return.

When for ten minutes or more he had been pacing to and fro on the same spot, he became aware of a deep cold within him, a cold driving through his anorak and his sweater to his flesh and the bones beneath. He had to move to keep warm, but in which direction? Best perhaps to go down, to find the camp again . . .

And then he stood still. At his feet, rough grass and boulders, showing dimly through the mist. But no path. A moment's panic drove through him. In those minutes of walking to and fro for warmth, he'd strayed from the path. But not far, surely; it couldn't be far? He'd only moved a little way . . . but to left or right? . . .

Well, he'd soon find out. He had only to try both, and he was bound to find it again. This way . . . here? No, merely more stones and rough grass; featureless. Perhaps a little higher; perhaps he'd moved downwards . . .

He was climbing again. Further into the mist, and still no sight or sound of them . . . He paused. Absurd to have these twinges of panic when he must be so near home. He had to keep from his mind the towering images of the Pyrenean heights, for within this mist, unseen, they made his head spin. Not far. Not far to go. He had only to find the path . . .

He listened. Was there not a different sound, something other than the wind? Softly through the mist came the purl and rush of water: a stream. He felt a lift of heart. He had only to find that, follow that, and it would lead him down to the valley again. Follow a stream bed when you're lost: climbing-lore, learned long ago.

But where exactly was that sound of water coming from? He strained to listen. From his right, he thought: a little higher. He climbed again across the misty ground more sure now that he had a purpose. If he could find the stream . . . He went on, listening for the sound of water; listening too for the sound of voices, for Howard's voice, bellowing across the mountain slopes and the mist . . . he wasn't over-fond of Howard, but how welcome that sound would be!

On, then. With a little less confidence, because the sound of the stream, which had been faint but clear, now seemed to be diminished. He turned, then stood uncertain. For the first time he felt entirely lost, having now moved far from the original path. He had only the guidance of the water, which seemed further off than before.

It was then that he saw the path. Even through the curdling mist it showed clear: a path between grass and boulders. He bounded towards it with grateful energy. Confidence had returned to him. Howard and Crawley, Fenstone, Vernon and Merryweather ... soon he would see them again.

§

Howard, his face raw from open weather, his anorak shining, led four wet and breathless boys down with heavy boot-treads to the camp. Here the mist lay in patches, and Gene Carson waited, on the look-out.

Howard wiped his face. He said, 'O.K., you win. It's a bloody awful day.'

Gene said sharply, 'What goes?'

Howard was breathing heavily. Merryweather began, 'We couldn't find——'

'Shut up. Let me explain.' Howard was out of temper as well as breath. 'Rutherford. Nigel. He got adrift from the rest of us.'

'*How*, in God's name?'

Howard wiped his face again, as if the edge on Carson's voice had stung him. 'I don't know. There was something up with him——'

'What d'you mean?'

'I tell you, I don't know. At first he went striding off, ahead of all the party. I called him back and gave him a talking to. He seemed to be thinking of something else. Dreamy. *Then* he began to lag behind, and I had to shout at him again to keep together. He still seemed in a bit of a dream, but he did as he was told — at least, I *think* he did——'

'You *think*——'

'The mist came down. At first it was nothing much: a sort of cloudiness in the air. And ... I've just remembered, somewhere about then, there was a fork in the path. It's possible he turned the wrong way——'

'Didn't you take a roll-call?'

'A short while later, when the mist came all about us. It came so fast——'

'Mists in mountains usually do, or so I recall.'

104

Howard looked again as though the dry words had stung him. 'I called them all by name. I got them all together, except Rutherford. When I found he was missing, I began a search. I had to keep the boys with me——'

'Yes, I see you couldn't really risk losing another——'

'Dammit, he's not lost! Only wandered a little way off the path.'

Gene looked at the white walls of mist above them. 'You know as well as I do how simple it is to wander too far . . . to come to a precipice, get stuck on some unmanageable rock. The boy's lost, and we've got to treat it like that.'

'All right, I didn't say we hadn't.' Gene could see extreme anxiety on Howard's face, mixed with angry shame at being wrong about the weather, and the day.

Gene was fixing a helmet to his head with a lamp like a miner's on his forehead. 'You're pretty done in: seems to me best if I go up and see if I can trace him. Compass . . . whistle . . . might be a chance. Meanwhile, if you'll allow me to suggest — to my senior in this expedition — I think you should take a jeep down to Andorra La Vella, and get in touch with the police——'

'The police?'

'We can't take chances; you know that as well as I do. You'll find them — the *Policia* in a large building called *Central de Telecommunications* at the end of the main street, over the river——'

'Don't think we can count on them taking any action. Foreign policemen aren't like ours, in my experience.'

'Maybe not. But we have to start there. Just as we do at home. Maybe they'll put you on to the firemen, or some rescue group. They must have one: all mountain places do.'

'Back to that damned town? Can't I telephone from Massana, or one of those God-forsaken villages——'

'Ever tried to telephone a foreign police station on a foreign telephone?'

Howard grunted, gave a nod, and began to make his way to the jeep. The hunch of his shoulders and his weary but hastening walk, Gene thought, told of his disappointment and anxiety. 'Hi,' said Gene, 'you'd better take Mike Lester with you——' he thrust one of the boys forward: 'He's good at languages: don't know about Catalan, of course.'

Mike, a tall boy with ragged dark hair, pulled on his anorak with all the enthusiasm of one singled out for action. As they climbed into the jeep Howard called back, 'What happens if they don't understand a word we say?'

'You just roar at them until they find someone who does.'

The jeep sent its noise into the valley, and the mist. Gene watched them go. It had seemed the best thing to do; he kept his doubts to himself. Better in some ways if he'd gone down to Andorra La Vella. On the other hand he was rested and full of energy, whereas Howard was exhausted by the climb and the search, and his buried but palpable anxiety. Howard's readiness to accept his advice, Gene thought, sprang from that exhaustion and that fear.

No time to brood on Howard's prospects: Gene was packing his rucksack with a first-aid kit, flask, sweaters. He was talking as he worked: 'I'll have two of you with me; the rest stay here — and for mercy's sake *stay* here: warm yourselves up and wait for news. Who's coming with me? — a couple of fresh ones, I want; not you lot who've been through the laundry——'

'I'd like to come, sir.'

The voice surprised him. He had not expected Mark Stevens to volunteer for this; he had so far shown little relish for climbing. There had been — had there not? — a coolness between him and Nigel last night: no time to disentangle this now. 'O.K.; get ready fast. And for God's sake keep close. Got a whistle? And you, Cornwall? Oh, good.' He was happier with Cornwall, a snub-nosed boy who'd won the high jump in the school sports, and took life with a solid calm. 'We're going a little way up the path. Not too far; the far stuff'll have to be left for the experts. But there's a chance we may be lucky — yes, Stevens, what is it?'

Mark Stevens was not himself this morning, Gene noticed, the cloud of preoccupation on his face. He said, 'Nigel's boots are there.'

'What the hell d'you mean?'

'His boots are there in the tent: I've just seen them.'

'Then what in God's name did he go out in? Bedroom slippers?'

'No, sir. I think he must be wearing those rubber and canvas shoes — they're quite thick——'

'But not, it would seem, quite as thick as he is — what in hell was he thinking of ?'

Stevens' head was down. 'I don't know.'

'Going out in gym shoes over the Pyrenees . . . must have been walking in his sleep.'

Stevens didn't reply.

Gene made a grimace of acceptance and said to the boys who were left behind, '*Keep where you are*. If Mr Howard comes back with the Andorran Police or the Fire Brigade or a band of merry men, all set for rescue, tell them where we've gone ... Come on, you two. I'll sound the whistle every now and again. When I do, we'll stop absolutely still and listen for a reply. Got that? O.K. Now for it.'

With the two boys following, he began to climb. The mist quickly drenched them, and behind the mist, like the deep echo of cannon shot, he heard the first beat of thunder.

§

Nigel continued to follow his path. He had a sensation of unease, because, though he'd been walking for some time, he hadn't come out of the mist, and he'd seen no sign of the camp. Should it not be near? He stood to listen, but could hear nothing. Nothing except a new sound, like distant explosions in a quarry.

On, down the path. Still the mist about him, and that undercurrent of sound, which must surely be distant thunder. Thunder? He remembered the cow-herd by the hut who had spoken of storm ... Was there a darkening of the air, or was it merely in his mind, because of these memories? He spurred himself on, slipping and stumbling over the stones.

It was only then, because one stone, jagged and upright, hurt his foot that he saw he wasn't wearing his boots, as Howard had instructed. He stood still for a moment, looking down at the canvas shoes with their thick rubber soles. Thick, but not thick enough to prevent the pain from a sharp stone. How had he not noticed this before? Perhaps because the heavy socks concealed them. And how had he been such a fool as to forget his boots? Just the muddle in his head this morning, the overtone of the quarrel with Mark: these had fogged his judgement and set him off unprepared.

Well, boots or no boots, Nigel thought, it didn't matter so much now, for he was back on the path, and though it seemed to be going on for a long time, soon it must bring him to the camp. He was limping with the pain of his foot, but he could get down; he wasn't badly hurt.

The sound of thunder came again, louder than before. Despite his limp, he went more quickly. He could feel the freshening wind and hear between the lion's roar of thunder the splash of water. The stream. He must be near now, for the stream had run close to the camp. He felt a glow of relief, and the added energy of one whose danger is almost past.

Never mind the poor shoes, nor the iron sound of thunder; go quickly. He'd almost made it, and would surely return to a welcome . . .

The change came so suddenly that for a moment he thought he was seeing some sort of mirage.

For the mist was moving off, showing great gaps of valley and mountainside; ripping and tearing away, building the country about him piece by piece, lifting like a physical weight from his eyelids; letting him see clear.

See the familiar steep and terraced mountains, the lower slopes wooded with birch and pine; and below him, at the end of the path, a little open valley——'

But no camp; no sign of the rest of his company; nothing but empty boulders and rough grass. His heart bounded once, then beat faster. He drew a hand over his eyes, but he had seen truly. The mist was gone, and he had come to the end of the path. But he could see only the steep fall of mountains, lifting to their great height; nothing else, not even a hut or a house, or an old church tower . . . Empty and dangerous country, and with this new strength of wind, as if they came in the train of the mist, clouds so dark that it seemed night must be contained within them, driving towards him like armies.

He stood still, oblivious to the small pain in his foot. He'd taken the wrong path — but in which direction? The mist robbed you of discernment, like being blindfolded and turned about in a game . . . he didn't know. He simply didn't know. He looked about him, trying to ignore the dark driving clouds and the louder beat of thunder. All the mountainsides with the downward smoke of their streams looked alike; he could see no feature anywhere that would define the place he had come to now. From the small clearing where he stood, the ground fell steeply away, showing no further sign of a path. Was he in Spain or France? He didn't know.

They must be looking for him — should he wait where he was? But the vast multiplication of the mountains became clear to him, and he saw how easy it would be for any party to search for a long time before they found him. Amongst the heights, and their great number, he felt very small.

And now the storm was coming — those black and whirling clouds let loose their rain, a sudden icy wall of water, blacking the air, chilling him, banishing again the world about him.

He had to move on, somehow find shelter. Beaten as with rods by the rain, he turned away from the path, across the wild mountainside. He was shivering now from the icy rain which seemed already, within a few minutes, to have found the weak parts of his anorak and soaked through to his skin. He needed another sweater, but he couldn't stop; he had to move on, to try to find shelter. The force of the rain seemed to batter everything out of his mind except the necessity to go on: he could feel the water running between his clothes, running down his skin. As he went, words that Gene had quoted swam through his mind: '*These mountains are full of vengeance and hate to be disturbed.*' What else had he told them? Of another climber who said, '*When you have made up your mind that you are lost, behave like a man in grave danger; wandering between the high valleys it is too easy to die from exhaustion.*'

He slipped and scurried, almost lost his balance. The ground had become an icy, running torrent; the rain had made of the dry ground a marshy river, and he went ankle-deep, his canvas shoes soaked and filthy, giving him little hold.

He had lost all sense of direction; he could only hope that he would come upon shelter, even if it were no more than an overhang of rock which would keep off the worst of the storm . . . Was there not the shape of one, a little way ahead? The rain so blinded him that he couldn't be sure, but if he could get there before the wall of icy water froze him and made him incapable of movement . . . He saw the shape more clearly, and began to run.

And as he did so, he slipped on the watery torrent of ground and fell heavily against a stone. Winded, he lay there, while the rain savaged him. Slowly he struggled to his feet — then gave a gasp of pain. The stab that went through his right foot was like a skewer of fire.

A broken bone? It might be: he couldn't tell. Comes from wearing these damned shoes, he thought; comes from being such a damned fool, getting off the path; comes from quarrelling with Mark; comes from . . .

The tired anger of his mind gave out. He had to move, however hard it was. He couldn't put his right foot to the ground; he must crawl.

That was just possible. The pain still goaded his foot, but he could move on all fours over the rushing muddy ground. No climb with his father had brought such force of rain, nor such cold . . .

As he went, he had the sensation that he was not alone. Some-one was close, perhaps close behind him. He turned his head, but could see nothing but the wall of rain. Yet he was aware that some-one shadowed him. Who? He said, 'Are you there?' as loudly as he could: no sound but the lash of rain and the drumbeatm close now, of thunder.

No one, then? But he was still aware of company; perhaps he was feverish or in a half-dream` . . . Certainly he had lost all sense of bearings, even of the other boys and Larry Howard. This com-pany that shadowed him was not of that kind. Was the memory of his father more than memory; was the pattern to repeat itself; was he near now to that moment of fear which his father had found on the Cumbrian hills?

He paused to ease the muscles of his back and to recover his breath. The pain in his foot was dulled by cold and the unyielding cataract of rain.

The words came to him again: ' . . . *behave like a man in grave danger . . .*' Nothing to do but to struggle further, in the hope per-haps of shelter, or that he would (miraculously, it seemed now) be found.

How long could he survive in this rain and this cold?

He wouldn't think about that. He couldn't know.

8

The late-September London day was cool but sunlit. It was a Saturday: a fine Saturday, Eve reflected, as she climbed the stairs and put her shopping-bag down in the kitchen.

The silence of the room met her with its accustomed force. She turned on the radio: did not hear the voice which altered the silence, nor identify the music; it was merely that she needed the vacuum to be filled, so that some part of her mind was dulled from thought.

She put away the tins, the packets, the cleaning powders. There was, she discovered, a small sense of achievement in doing things that did not really matter any more: tasks such as paying immediately the bills which came addressed to James Rutherford, Esq. She had tried to alter this to 'Mrs James Rutherford' but it seemed that the computer, no more than herself, was able to adjust to the fact that she was now a widow.

She glanced at the calendar on the wall. The calendar was reassuring, for there, printed clearly in black, was the date of Nigel's return. Less than a week now. For a few moments she let her mind dwell on his arrival; the blessed infusion of life into this place; the excited chatter of his voice; the traveller's tales.

Absently she looked from the kitchen window, at the first of autumn in the square. Autumn, herald to a winter of which she was afraid.

But of course if she had protested that the days of summer, full of other people's plans and excursions, thrust pain home, she couldn't complain of winter which kept them indoors ...

On the table in the living-room was a long letter from her solicitor, which explained her dubious financial future; another from her accountant which appeared to remove what was left, when the solicitor had done. The accountant sent indecipherable forms from the Inland Revenue which he said, not without compassion, required immediate reply. Her landlords added to this with a notice that they were applying to the Rent Officer for an increase in rent. All these letters must be dealt with: she took a cloth and began to clean the kitchen cooking-stove, which was easier than answering them.

When she'd finished cleaning the stove she decided to wash down the dresser. Nothing wrong in that, she told herself; anyone could clean a dresser without feeling guilt. She would attend to the letters later on; after all, the Saturday post had gone, and there was none till Monday now . . .

The sound of the telephone. She said, 'Hullo?'

'It's Ransome here: Giles Ransome.'

She could not think why Nigel's Headmaster, who lived in Derbyshire, should be telephoning her. His well-mannered voice said, 'I'd like to come and see you.'

Cold touched her, because any new thing had its element of fear, but she said only — 'Why, yes; of course. Where are you?'

'I'm in town.'

'Is your wife with you?'

'No, I came alone; I got an early train this morning. I'd like to come right away, if that suits you. I'll get a cab; it shouldn't take too long.'

Now her throat was dry, but she was unable to form any question. 'Yes, all right. I'll be here.'

'Good.'

Before she could say more he had put the telephone down.

She stood for some moments, with the echo of his voice in her head. 'It shouldn't take too long' — but of course that could mean anything. She had no idea where he was speaking from — Holland Park? Hampstead? Ealing? She'd had no time to ask him; indeed it had not occurred to her to do so.

Nothing to do now but wait. He would come: the urgency of his voice made that clear. But waiting was difficult, for she could set herself to no task, not even cleaning the dresser.

Giles Ransome arrived within half an hour. His arrival was better than waiting for him, though not much. She took his coat and led him into the living-room, where the letters lay scattered on the table.

One glance at his face with its spectacles and lean authority made it clear that he did not like his news. He shook his head at the offer of coffee or a drink. Nor did he sit down, but turned to look out of the window as if he waited for someone, though of course there was no one else to come; just the two of them here, both standing as if at some ceremony.

He said, 'I'm sorry to descend on you with so little warning.'
She shook this away. He went on, 'I've had some news from
Andorra. Rather disturbing news, I'm afraid.'

She stood, cold now; merely waiting.

'I don't want you to be unduly worried. I'm quite sure it'll be all
right——'

She made no sound.

'I've had a message from Howard: he managed to get through
to me on the telephone last night. I'm afraid Nigel is . . . just temporarily . . . lost from the rest of them.'

'*Lost?*'

She saw the glance he gave her, perhaps afraid of what was to
come. 'It seems a mist came down, and Nigel got separated——'

'I don't understand.' (She'd said this before; before when
Jamie . . .) '*When* did Nigel get lost?'

'Yesterday——'

'You mean he's been out in those mountains all *night*?'

'Howard thinks he must've gone down into the wrong valley——'

'I don't care what Howard thinks. How did Nigel get lost? He
knows about mountains — he's climbed with . . . with his
father——'

'I don't know. I don't know all the details. Howard was telephoning from Andorra; the line was pretty bad.'

She drew in her breath, trying to take control. She thought This
can't be happening; the thing you fear beyond all reason doesn't
come to pass, just in the way you feared it.

He went on, watching her with care, 'Gene Carson and two
other boys went at once on a search party; Howard went down to
Andorra La Vella to alert the police. Howard had to find an inter-
preter; trouble is, the chap turned out to be a press man, so we're
going to have them on our tail——'

'I don't give a damn about the press!'

'You're bound to be upset   '

'*Upset.* Oh, you don't know; you truly don't know . . .' She took
another breath, to check this fear and anger. Across the gulf of
this dark moment she could remember Giles Ransome and his
wife: a man of some unhappiness . . .

She said, 'I'm sorry. Perhaps you do know. Perhaps you have
some idea . . . In any case, it was good of you to come and tell me.
All I know is, I must get out there.'

113

'*Go there* ..? But why? There's nothing you can do: every-thing's being done, will be done——'

'You don't understand,' she said, but quietly now. 'I have to go there. When ... when Jamie fell, I wasn't with him——'

'Andorra's one hell of a place to get at——'

'I know about Andorra; I've been there, with Jamie: we drove over those mountains, along that road——'

'It's a day's journey——'

'What's a day? I must go. Somehow. It can't be impossible——'

He drew a hand across his forehead. 'No, I don't suppose any-thing is impossible. But I think it's a waste of ... energy, I sup-pose. By the time you get there, he'll be found——'

'You can't know. I just have to be there.'

His eye went over her, as if he summed up the measure of her resolution. 'Very well. If you must. But I maintain it's an inadvis-able thing to do.'

'I daresay.' She was into her bedroom for her coat, shoes, bag. 'Nearly everything I've done since Jamie's death has been inadvis-able. If not worse.' She returned, dressed for the street. 'There's a travel agency not far from here; Jamie and I used to book our holi-days there ...'

'I'll come with you.'

She didn't know that this was what she wanted, but since she had given him little but the unwelcome usually accorded the bringer of bad news, she could not refuse him. Indeed, as she walked with him she found herself glad of his steady masculine pace beside her.

The travel agency, flying its bright flags of holiday brochures, appeared entirely incongruous. A well-dressed woman was book-ing a winter cruise to the Caribbean. When Eve said she wanted to leave for Andorra today, the young man behind the counter said, 'Today?' but it was clearly part of his travel-side manner to show surprise at nothing and he threshed through catalogues and time-tables with expert speed. As he did so her eye fell upon a mid-day newspaper, and the small heading (there were of course in today's world larger events) *Schoolboy missing in Spain: Police alerted.*

She swung to Giles Ransome. 'How can they know so soon?'

'I told you. Howard, and the press chap. News travels fast these days. And any trouble with school exploits is good copy——' he broke off. 'Well, there's always a band of people who say we shouldn't let them go.'

She didn't answer, as the young man was talking of planes and times of flight. 'Trouble is, I can't guarantee the connection. It's late in the season . . . There's just this one chance——'

('An *outside* cabin; my husband insists on it.')

The young man was now telephoning. She read the newspaper paragraph; it said little she didn't know, and did not mention Nigel by name. '. . . Mr Howard, Housemaster at Westerfield and leader of the expedition said, "We have every hope of finding him."' She let this go, while the young man, still speaking into the telephone, turned timetables with one hand. He seemed to be encountering difficulty, and of a sudden she feared that the journey might not be possible after all——

The young man was saying, 'Is your passport in order?'

She thought quickly. 'Yes.'

'Can you be at Gatwick by three?'

She glanced at the clock on the wall. Noon. She said, 'Yes,' again. She saw Giles Ransome glance at her. No, none of this was quite sane. But he hadn't been there, not to the place of despair, of featureless dark. She would like to have explained this but there was no time.

The young man said, writing quickly, 'There's a cancellation on a flight leaving this afternoon. From Gatwick to Perpignan. Then a tourist coach, over the French pass into Andorra. You won't get there till the early hours, I'm afraid——'

'Never mind.'

Ticket in hand, explanations in her head she stood outside, briefly, with Giles Ransome. He said, 'You know where the camp is?'

Yes, Nigel had told her; had even drawn a map. For a moment Ransome's face, lean, careworn, printed itself on her mind, and she saw the problems that would attend him after the press announcement: the assault of radio and television; accusations of carelessness, inadequate precautions . . .

She had time to be sorry for him as she said goodbye; but this was quickly lost in impatience to be on with the journey, to be gone.

§

At the camp, Gene Carson saw little change. The storm of the evening before had like all storms abated, but now the mist had returned and a thin drizzle crept down in a cold persistent silence, as if it would never stop.

Howard banged his hands together and said, 'I don't believe he's lost. I just don't believe it.'

Gene said, 'You reckon?'

Howard said forcibly, 'Yes, I reckon.'

'He's been out all night.'

'He could have found shelter.'

'Just possible. But even so——'

'I tell you, nothing could have happened to that boy. He knew all about mountains; his father was——'

Gene said, 'We all know who his father was.'

Howard drew his hand over his face. '*Nothing* could have happened to him. He'll be found. One of these damned dagoes——'

'I should be careful how you talk of them: our lives — or rather, Nigel Rutherford's — depend on their goodwill.'

Out of the mist, a short, broad-shouldered man, swarthy-faced, came towards them. He wore a padded anorak, climbing boots and bright orange socks pulled up over the ends of shabby corduroy trousers. His companions came behind him, carrying ropes. They were all dark, with complexions burned by some now vanished sun. The leader, Luis Madero, the only one who spoke English, said, 'I'm afraid — so far — nothing. We must try other valleys; if he has took a wrong path he could have gone down one hundred different ways.'

Gene said, 'Then somehow we must get to all the valleys.'

'Ah — *si* — we do our best. Also we pray to *Nuestra Señora da Meritxell*, the Holy Virgin of Meritxell, also to *Sant Antoni*; his shrine is close to here.'

Gene said, 'Pray all you like.'

Howard interrupted, 'For God's sake, we can't waste time *praying*——'

Gene grinned, and said, 'For *God's* sake?', while Luis Madero looked sadly at Howard: 'Here in Andorra we have great faith in the *Mare de Déu* — the Mother of God. In this small country there have been many miracles.'

'Well, we certainly need one now,' Gene said.

'*Déu sa bono.*' Luis crossed himself. 'We will find ... But we need for it to change — *el tiempo* — He glanced upwards. 'If the weather will change, there is the helicopter. No, there is none in Andorra, but we can get from France — *Centre de Vol en Mon-*

116

tagne. Between Bourg-Madam and Mont-Louis: within range. But in this weather, impossible. Impossible to fly.' He glanced again upwards, at the enveloping mist. 'Now we search the Spanish frontier. Easy to cross into Spain: you will know that smugglers are all the time taking cognac and tobacco over the borders.'

Gene nodded, and looked at his map. At least, he said, he and his colleague could do something——

Luis followed the contours on Gene's map with a blunt finger. 'If you and the Señor will take the road towards El Serrat. Follow the road in your jeep, through Ordino, Cortinada and Llorts.'

'Looks to be a long way in the wrong direction,' said Howard.

Luis shrugged. 'In *la neblina* — mist — he may have gone anywhere.'

Gene said, 'We're in your hands'; and Howard gave a grunt, as if he agreed, but would rather it were not so.

Climbing into the jeep, Gene cast one look at the group of Andorran men as they slung their rucksacks and, with few words, began their climb. Strangers, yet doing what they could to find a boy from a school far off.

Howard said, 'I'll drive. I know that damn road.'

Gene nodded, perceiving that Howard needed to restore in himself some sense of leadership. He drove in brooding silence until he said, 'Of course they'll find him.'

Gene didn't reply.

'When I was at the police station,' Howard went on, 'the chap who did the interpreting — the press chap — told me there were very few accidents in Andorra. There was this damn road, and you had only to get back to the road.'

'Yeah; maybe.' Clear how great was Howard's need to hang on to this hope. But Gene saw not only the road but the interminable valleys, the depth and height of the mountains that guarded them. Anywhere. Any path, mule track, smugglers' way, leading without purpose into the mist.

Howard said, 'That press chap started asking questions. About how the boys were equipped. Whether they had the right clothes, compasses and all that.'

'I hope you told him yes.'

'I said — to the best of my knowledge. Rutherford was being a bit of a nuisance, as you know. I didn't check that he had everything; he's not an infant; I'd briefed them the night before . . . But whatever happens, I shall be answerable to Ransome——'

'And he, like Ministers (Government, I mean; not the Cloth) will have to carry the can. Headmasters always do.'

Howard gave a groan. 'Oh God, yes; there'll be hell to pay. Hell. Someone must find him: those dagoes — or us. Someone *must*.'

Yes, indeed, Gene thought; but ... He said, 'And his mother ...'

'Dear God, yes; she came to see me, back at the school.' A sad longing showed on his face, as if he thought of the school where he was safe from such hazards as surrounded him here. 'I suppose she'll know by now.'

'Ransome would have to tell her.'

'What the hell do we *do*——?'

Gene shrugged. 'Our best. With luck, the weather may clear. It changes suddenly in these parts.'

Howard received this in silence, as the jeep turned, looped and climbed. He said at last, 'But he's been out all night. And it was cold.'

Gene didn't answer. He could see the mountains held in massive cold and dark, and Nigel alone, somewhere. Cold was the enemy. He wondered if it would win.

9

The window was in the wrong place. Puzzled, Eve stared at it, until sense and knowledge returned to her.

Words first of all: *I'm afraid Nigel is just temporarily lost from the rest of them.*

Not possible; not true; something she had dreamed of, in that time after Jamie's death . . .

But this was real. This strange hotel room in Andorra La Vella; the day before, which had begun with trivial shopping in the London street (just as that other day had begun quietly in the Rosthwaite Hotel) had so twisted and turned itself that she had travelled across Europe, and over the passes of the Pyrenees, arriving here in the small hours, in the dark and drenching rain.

Out of bed. Her body and mind still bruised by the long journey, like something which still continued. Gatwick, where voices were quiet, as if this were some place of alien worship; the punctual woman's voice on the loudspeaker disembodied, as the voice of an oracle should be; then the flight above dazzling clouds — a short respite, because one was far from the earth. Then the long, almost endless coach drive over the Pyrenees, first through the small towns and villages of France — Prades, Villefranche-de-Conflent — where women in black were seated in the sunless day outside their houses on wooden chairs and watched impassively as the coach drove through. A pause at Mont-Louis beyond Fontpédrouse, at a large unwelcoming café, hurried and barefloored, from whose windows she could see the mountain heights, blurred with rain and cloud . . . Light going from the day as they travelled on, so that the mountain peaks loomed more darkly, with at some distance, between cloud, the little flush of coral sunset on snow . . . A change of weather, she had thought? It might be . . .

Now she scrambled to the window, undid the shutters, and stared at the discovered landscape. The crowded blue slate, 'fishscale' roofs of the town below her, mountain slopes beyond. The rain had ceased, but the slopes climbed into cloud and the air was cold.

Only now did she know how deeply she had hoped for that clarity of morning which could so often follow bad mountain weather. She had hoped for sun, for warmth, for that festival of good things which is on the edge of thought for those in sorrow or fear: the longing, after the effort and the pain, for a gilded answer, a promise that all will be well.

Childish, of course; that wasn't how things worked. Those clouds hung low; and all last night, it seemed, the sky had slung down its icy Pyrenean rain . . .

. . . just temporarily lost . . .

Hurriedly, she washed and dressed. Useless to say, God wouldn't take Nigel as well as Jamie: God could do anything that seemed best to him . . . What else had Jamie quoted to her? 'Where there is sorrow, there is holy ground.' Yes, maybe that's true, indeed I can see how it might be, that it's good to carry a cross, but I don't want holy ground, I don't want a cross, not any more: I want Nigel, alive, restored, not lost from the rest of them . . .

She glanced again to the mountain slopes.

I don't know why I've come, she thought; I can do no good: I can't climb these mountains alone and I can't look for him. And as for Jamie, look as far as I can, I can never find him again . . . Yet, she thought, when he was alive, the few times we were parted, I used to think of him far away, and I didn't like the distance: now he isn't far off or near; wherever I am he is no further off . . . so perhaps it makes sense to say to him Please help; please help them find him.

She went downstairs and at once to the reception desk. Instead of the sleepy concierge of the early hours, there was now an alert man of middle age. She asked if he spoke English; he shrugged and looked as if this were more than could be expected of him.

'Perhaps I can help you?'

Eve turned to see a woman of about fifty dressed in a frock of full-length, shabby round the hem, a windcheater and sandals on bare feet. (Some echo of Belinda here? But this woman's face, small and pretty, had also a look of sharp intelligence.)

Eve looked at her with a kind of love, and a familiarity which she could not quite explain. This woman seemed the first force of good which she had so far discovered. Eve said, 'I want to know if there's any news of my son.' She explained about the expedition, and produced Nigel's map which she carried like a talisman. 'I was

travelling all yesterday, and part of the night. No one knew anything when I arrived. There might be news.'

She caught in the woman's face an authentic sympathy. 'Ah — I
will ask.'

She spoke to the man who listened impassively, giving one swift
glance towards Eve, and then back to her companion.

He shrugged again, and answered in his own language.

The woman turned to Eve. 'He says he knows nothing of any
accident, or loss. He says he is desolated that such a thing should
happen to the son of the Señora, but he finds it hard to
believe——'

'But it's *true*——' Eve said, desperate now, because the man's
disbelief seemed to put up a wall against hope.

The woman beside her said, 'Yes, of course it is — what's your
name? . . . good: mine's Carrie: Carrie Morgan. Mrs, I suppose
you'd say, though I've not seen my husband for many years.' She
turned away from the reception desk, a hand on Eve's arm. 'The
Andorrans have a great pride in their country. Since it's only
about the size of Greater London, this is understandable. And
since they depend on tourists for their prosperity, their motto is,
of course, that there are no accidents in Andorra — it's too small.'

'But he's missing——'

'I know; I know. But the hotel proprietor doesn't want to. We'll
have to find someone who does——' she looked at her watch,
which resembled a schoolboy's watch, on her bony wrist.'I have to
meet a friend here; I'm expecting him at any moment. I suggest
you go to the tourist office; it's only a short distance from here —
have you had any breakfast?'

'No, I don't want it.'

'All the same——' Carrie Morgan seemed to have taken command, and led Eve to one of the tables and made her sit down
opposite two burnished young women, one dark, one copper-
haired, who gave her youthful, energetic smiles.

Carrie explained Eve's purpose; their smiles vanished and they,
like Carrie herself, seemed genuinely distressed. Their names, Carrie said, were Bridget (the dark one; she was a nurse); and June
(who was a social worker). They were on a walking tour all the
way from St Jean de Luz, but the weather had turned against
them.

'You can say that again.' Bridget had the glow of any young
woman who spends all the time she can in the open air. 'Terribly

121

sorry about your son, but I'm sure he'll be all right. If we can help——'

'Sure,' said June, who wore a green polo-necked sweater and had the open intelligence of one who is used to dealing with people in trouble. 'Andorra's not that large. Have some coffee, even if you can't eat.'

Carrie sat beside them and explained about the tourist office. 'The *Sindicat d'Iniciativa de los Valles d'Andorra*. The Señora there speaks good English. If she has news, she will tell you. It may be good news: Such things do happen, in spite of all evidence to the contrary.' Together with Bridget and June she offered to come to the office, but Eve, though warmed by this, said Thank you, but she'd rather go alone.

On the steps of th hotel, Carrie Morgan directed her to the *Sindicat d'Iniciativa*. 'I have a car,' Carrie Morgan said, pointing to what seemed to Eve the oldest car she had seen for a long time: dented and rusted, it looked ready for the scrap-heap. 'It may come in useful later on ... Good luck!'

As Eve hurried to the *Sindicat* she could feel, like the gift of warmth from a brazier in a cold street, the kindness of Carrie, and of Bridget and June. This she had not expected; certainly not in this town, which was a paradox of fine mountains and cheap shops selling liquor and gaudy Spanish dolls.

But at the *Sindicat*, a touch of remembered nightmare entered in. A young woman said haltingly that the Señora who spoke good English was not there. When would she return? A shrug. Impossible to say. Perhaps this afternoon.

Had she heard, Eve asked, of an accident: a boy lost in the mountains?

A shake of the head. 'Here in Andorra we do not have——'

'I know, I know; you don't have accidents. Well, there's been one now. And I want *news* ... Do you speak French?'

'*Oui, mais je ne sais rien.*' It would be best, the young woman went on, half in French, half in English, if Eve went to the police. Here was the address. She wrote it down.

Out again into the noisy street, but with less hope and greater fear. Across the bridge, and over the fast and frothing waters of the Valira. A tall modern building, offering small comfort, cut off, it seemed, like most official places from the disarray of humanity.

The *Policia*. On the third floor. As at the *Sindicat*, a blank wall of incomprehension. She spoke in French to a dark young man in fawn uniform. He frowned at a pencil held between his hands.

'*Vous avez dit — Arinsal?*'

She lost her French and said, 'That's where the camp was——'

'*Je crois qu'un des garçons s'est perdu——*'

'*Is* there any news? Has he been found?'

'*Je ne sais rien.*'

She turned and ran down the stairs without waiting for the lift.

§

Now all she wanted was to find Carrie Morgan again, and the two girls, who had shown concern, and could understand her when she spoke.

She found them all together; and with them a man of perhaps sixty with plentiful grey hair and a beard. He had the good looks of one who has gained rather than lost with age: sadness somewhere, but a mouth with a turn of humour. She saw the pinned and empty sleeve of his left arm. When Carrie said, 'Any news?' Eve could not for a moment answer, being breathless with running and fear. She shook her head.

The man said, 'My name is Benedict. Benedict Lang. I've heard your story. I would beg you not to lose hope.'

'We have an idea,' Carrie said. 'I will drive you up to the camping ground. Oh, it will not be at all difficult. Benedict will come with us. Benedict knows these parts well — he'll explain why. Bridget and June will stay near the hotel, in case news comes here. Sit down: you look as if you need to.'

Still breathless Eve sat with them. Not only Carrie's face, but the faces of the three others were in some way familiar . . . yet they were strangers: she had never seen them before. Puzzled, she said, 'I don't know why you should be so kind.'

Carrie said she didn't think it was kind to help someone in such obvious distress. Benedict Lang said, 'Rutherford? Mrs Jamie Rutherford, did I hear? . . . Ah. One of my heroes. A tremendous loss. I read of his death with that sadness which perhaps only the middle-aged can know. But you doubtless hear such tributes often.'

'Some people remember him, and I'm so glad when they do. But I think people forget quickly. The ranks close up: the person isn't there any more: that's all.'

He gave her a look of level compassion. 'Yes, I understand. In the old days, when the young men died . . . But we've no time for the past. Old men don't so much forget as remember with advantages . . . do we go to the camp?'

The car which Carrie drove out of the noisy shopridden town bounded and clattered like a dust-cart. Carrie talked cheerfully over this sound, driving fast and with (it seemed to Eve) miraculously protected abandon. 'Benedict knows these parts so well,' she said, 'because he was in the Civil War. In the International Brigade. When the Republicans were defeated, he escaped over one of the passes of Andorra into France——'

'Leaving,' Benedict said, 'so many behind that in a way I had loved, and should not see again. I knew Spain before the war; as a young man I went from Aragon to Andalucia: I walked the streets of Cadiz, and felt the wind of Africa blow through the streets of Algeciras . . . I even went with my "scallop shell of quiet" on a pilgrimage to Compostella, though I found the Spanish mixture of blood and virgins, macabre miracles and relics sometimes too much for my taste.'

'Oh, I don't mind relics at all,' said Carrie Morgan, changing gear with a sound like splintering wood. 'One of St Peter's sandals, a bone of Moses, a hair from Mary Magdalene's head, a thorn from Christ's crown . . .'

'But how can a piece of bone, for goodness' sake, be of the slightest use? A piece of soul, perhaps, but no one as far as I know has been able to take a slice of that.'

Carrie made a sharp turn above a perpendicular drop with no concern. 'The older I get, the less I believe anything is nonsense. We deal with a material world. You have toes and fingernails——'

'Good God, they aren't relics!'

'No, but if you were a saint——'

'I'm not.'

'No, but if you *were*, some hundreds of years hence, people might reverence them——'

'What a perfectly disgusting idea.'

'I see no harm. What forces are there, of which we know nothing?' As they passed, at speed, a lurching wooden shrine Carrie raised one hand in salute; Eve had time to see the small faded figure of a Virgin and a few withered flowers.

Carrie, both hands on the wheel again, said, 'Don't think we've forgotten you. That salute was in hope for your son. We're in a country where savage events mix with a faith of enormous, yet often childish, proportions. This is a place where the violence of living is shot through by the mysteries, sometimes themselves violent, of another order of time . . . would you not agree, Benedict?'

'Oh, yes; I'm not arguing that.' As they passed another shrine he lifted his one arm. 'I will add my offering . . . At La Massana we take the road to the left, to Arinsal.'

The name, though of a place unknown, was familiar now, a symbol of danger. She wanted and did not want to find the place, to have an answer. From the window of the rattling and inelegant car, she could see that the mist still held. The road turned and climbed again.

They must be near now.

Carrie parked the car on a grass verge, where the land widened from its narrow defile. As Eve got out of the car, she thought of Rosthwaite, the last time she had been in mountain country . . .

And it was suddenly as she stood in the cold high misty air that she felt not the companionship of Carrie Morgan and Benedict Lang, but for one moment of Jamie, not a presence, perhaps, but a touch, a whisper out of the dark.

Then it was gone.

'I think,' Benedict said, 'I can see a jeep, up there to the left.'

They began to walk together, Eve going hurriedly ahead. It occurred to her that they must appear a strange company.

She saw first the bright orange anorak of Larry Howard. He was talking to a tall young man, who must be Gene Carson. A group of boys stood about them.

Boys, some of whom she knew, Mark among them.

But not Nigel.

No thoughts now; she went towards Larry Howard and Carson.

They both turned. She didn't like the way they looked at her: Gene Carson narrowed his eyes, heavy from lack of sleep; Howard stared at her as if she were a bad dream come true. He didn't ask how she came to be there at the camp.

She said, 'Nigel?'

Howard said, 'I'm afraid we haven't found him yet.'

She took extreme hold. 'Then he's been out two nights.'

Howard nodded heavily. He looked miserable, as if she were about to pour wrath on him, but she had no heart for that. Indeed, he aroused pity. She asked, 'What's happening?'

Gene Carson said, 'The Andorran rescue boys have been out, all day yesterday, and again today. So have Larry and myself. The weather's been against us. But our friend here, Luis, says there's hope of change.'

She saw Luis now, a broad-shouldered Catalan, weary and mud-stained. He did not have to be told who she was. He wiped his face which was scarred with fatigue and dirt, then gave a small bow. 'It is so — *el tiempo* will be better. Wind has changed.'

'But when the change comes — will it be too late?'

For a moment in the cold mountain place they were all silent, as if her question had put a spell on them, and the only sound was the river travelling fast.

Then Luis said, 'We have still . . . *esperanzas* . . . hopes.'

'It's been so cold.'

'We believe,' Howard said, 'that he had food and warm drink with him.'

'But two nights?'

Luis said again, 'We have hope.'

'When will the weather change?'

'Perhaps tonight. Perhaps tomorrow, in morning——'

'That would mean another night——'

'Perhaps.'

'It would be too much. No one could . . .'

She drew her hands over her face, but she was not weeping. There were these weary anxious men; there were Benedict and Carrie Morgan; there was this late harsh memory, this dark bridge so recently crossed. Yet there was this new thing within her, like the warmth from strong drink; a little spasm of courage, of determination not entirely to give way. She had made this perhaps useless journey, but now that she was here, she must do her best. She had, after all, been given the unexpected friendship of Carrie and Benedict, Bridget and June. She had the help of these men, sleepless and dirt-stained, who would look for Nigel till there was no hope left.

She would not think of the end of hope.

Benedict spoke to Luis; returned to say, 'I offered to go with them, but a one-armed bandit like me is likely they tell me — politely — to be more of a nuisance than anything else.' He looked up to the heights above them. 'Familiar ground . . . old familiar ground.' His eyes appeared to dwell on that past when the defeated men struggled and sometimes died in the passes and the snows.

Carrie said, 'They're going out again now.'

Eve nodded, and sat down on a boulder, for of a sudden strength seemed to have left her. There stayed in her mind this strange confliction, like a double-image: the memory of Borrowdale, the drive to the hospital, the farewell service in the valley churchyard in such weather as this; and now this moment of different fear.

She looked up to see that Mark was standing near her. He too looked tired and shaken, not the young man of oblique disparagement any more: the skin below his eyes darkened with fatigue, his hair blown, his face pinched with cold. He said, 'I'm sorry.'

She looked up at him in silence.

He said, 'I did go to look for him. With Mr Carson. We looked all day.'

She said, 'That was good.'

'I think it was because we quarrelled ... Nigel and me.'

'Quarrelled?'

He rubbed his already matted hair. 'I think so. He was all over the place the next morning, the day he ... got lost.'

'Why did you quarrel?'

'Oh, well; it was a silly thing. I suppose quarrels nearly always are. I didn't like the cable-car — I was scared of it, I mean, and that made me cross.'

'What on earth has that to do with anything?'

He gave her a glance of mixed apology and fatigue. 'I suppose I made it clear that I didn't care for any of this outdoor stuff. Well, I don't. And then you came into it——'

'*I* did? How?'

'He went on about how you hadn't wanted him to go, and we began to quarrel——'

He had her full attention now.

'I said things — well, you know how it is when you're angry. He knew you didn't want him to come and he got in a tangle about it, and in the end I wasn't speaking to him. I daresay he didn't sleep much; he was late getting up. I could see he was going to be late, but I didn't wake him ...'

She lost his voice. *He knew you didn't want him to come.* So events followed their pattern: her feverish concern that Nigel shouldn't go to Andorra had in the end played its part in his wandering from the path, and in this time now, when she waited.

Once you build badly, she thought, there's no end; it all goes

127

out of your control.

She looked up at Mark, deprived of his weapons of wit and mockery. She said, 'You've heard the wind's changing?'

'Yes.'

Neither of them spoke of two nights on the mountain. Neither of them said more. But her eyes followed him as he turned away; a young man meeting perhaps for the first time a circumstance too large for him.

He knew you didn't want him to come.

She must try to put those words out of her head, as their persistence could serve no purpose now.

Carrie Morgan was beside her. It would be better, Carrie said, to go back to the hotel and wait there for news.

Eve looked up, dumb with pleading. She did not know what was best; she only knew that she wanted to be here, as close to Nigel as she could. She said, 'I want to know — right away. When — when anything happens. They said the wind was changing——'

Benedict said, 'The rescuers are in radio contact with the police.'

'The police aren't any good. They don't speak English.'

'They would immediately get in touch with the hotel.'

'The man there isn't any good either.'

Benedict accepted the childish replies with calm. 'He would tell us. It would only take a few minutes.'

Yes; it would be sensible; she was doing no good here, sitting on a stone high in the hills, waiting for the mist to clear, waiting for the rescue party to return, waiting for . . .

'If you don't mind,' she said, 'I want to stay. At least until dark. If you want to go back . . .'

She was surprised how little argument was presented to her. It seemed that Carrie and Benedict were staying too. Someone brought a rug, and someone else brewed coffee. She felt strangely pampered; perhaps it was like this to be ill, very ill, without knowing it, perhaps dying, so that all the comforts were given you when you didn't expect, or seem to deserve them.

Until dark, she had said. How long before dark? The Catalan was gone with his men. The mist still formed and re-formed over the heights. Time slipped away, not fast or slow. (I seem to be nothing to do with time, she had said to Jamie's father; that was true now.)

Carrie Morgan (in stockings of bright plaid, a corduroy skirt and heavy climbing boots) sat beside her and ate a sandwich. Benedict crouched on the other side, took a flask of whisky from his pocket and drank deeply. Carrie said, 'You drink too much,' and Benedict wiped his mouth and gave a brief laugh. 'Have you ever seen me drunk? No. I drink for the same reason that I come back to Spain, and shall do, till my time is done. I drink because of the past.'

'Oh, the past,' said Carrie. 'We could all drink because of that.'

Their words went on, just touching her mind. Was the air darkening? With storm, perhaps ... No, it was the first of evening. Soon the day with its little hope would be gone.

Three nights?

No one could survive three nights.

The sound of foreign voices, loud and weather-torn, a stirring amongst the company cut into her thought.

Luis Madero stood before her. Useless to ask if he had good news. He said, 'Mist still there. We rest for a time, until is clear.'

Nothing to be said to that; of course he and his sleepless men must rest; she could ask no more of them.

When Carrie again said it would be best to return to the hotel, Eve got to her feet. Yes, she was ready to go back, because now she had little hope. Some, yes; you kept hope to the end; but three nights ... If she had obeyed her impulse it would have been to go running into the fortress of hills, into the mist, running and searching, calling his name ... But that, of course, would gain nothing: what had Jamie written? ... 'The Maladeta Massif ... the Cursed Mountains: how well the Spaniards name their terrible hills!'

Back down the dusky road. Here were the shadowed lopsided shrines with their withered flowers, and she thought, well they didn't do any good; nothing was any good. Carrie and Benedict were silent and the road grew darker. Lights from the villages as they passed spoke of that tranquil hour when it is better to be indoors. The car travelled at its usual speed: as Carrie took the sharp bends, Eve wondered whether, in the dark, they might not miss them and plunge to the valley below. No more waiting for news, no more fear ...

She must still have hope, because she wanted to reach the hotel; she wanted to know what happened when the wind changed; she wanted to know the end of the story.

And after that, if it did not go well?

She would not think further. She would watch the travelling and turning road.

§

Later, she sat with Carrie and Benedict, Bridget and June, over the dinner table. They had long finished their meal, and a few plates, crumbs and near-empty glasses stood to hand. Candles burned on the table, and Eve remembered the candles on the table of the Stevens' house which seemed now a world away. It was possible, in this quiet room (no one but themselves was left) with the pulse of candle-light to find some sort of ease. She looked at her companions, Carrie Morgan, Benedict, Bridget and June, with wonder because they had shared this time with her, when she had come to this place as a stranger. Was there some final mercy, when you came to the rim of the dark?

Bridget finished a piece of cheese and said, 'You mustn't think, because we eat a lot we don't feel for you. All nurses eat when they get the chance.'

Carrie said, 'Time was when I used to eat. Constantly. Biscuits and buns. That was when my husband left me, years ago, when I was quite young.' Her pointed, alert face looked beyond the elaborate decorations of this foreign dining-room, beyond the candles. 'I was surprised when it happened because of being young and as it seemed to me then, quite attractive. If he'd gone *now* . . . but then if we'd stayed together till now, perhaps had children, it might all have been quite different; one can't, of course, know.' She looked briefly into her glass, as if the possibilities of years showed there, with their unfathomable events, their unborn children.

Then she looked up, alert again. 'However, that was not so. We had no children, and he went off with a silly but kindly girl. So in the end, I took to travel. Some women take lovers, others eat and (certainly) drink, but I travel. All over the place in that car, and earn my living by writing about the places I go to. I seldom stay in hotels; I usually blow up my Lilo and sleep under a pine tree, or whatever sort of tree is indigenous to the parts I'm in. It makes a reasonable life.' She looked at Eve and smiled. 'I've not forgotten that you're waiting. But you don't have to listen to anything we say.'

'Oh yes; I'm listening.' Indeed this was true, for although at every movement behind her, at every sound of the distant tele-

130

phone she turned her head in passionate hope, she was able to absorb the words these people spoke. Their talk was offered it seemed in compassion, and she received it so.

Benedict said, 'Oh, well . . . I turned to this.' He refilled his glass from a bottle of whisky which the waiter had put on the table. 'My wife died some years ago, but it wasn't her death that made me drink, much though I loved her. It began when I came back without this — ' he tapped the empty sleeve — 'from the Spanish War. Of course there've been more terrible things since . . . if you can quantify suffering: I don't know if you can. But for me that was the true time of fire, of seeing the young men die. One particularly, whom I loved. Oh, I don't mean in the modern or ultimate sense. In war, in the climate of sudden and senseless death, men love each other.'

The dining-room had quietened; sound from the kitchens came faintly as if the activity of the evening was nearly done. Outside the steep slopes were lost in the dark, removed from this space of candlelight . . . she would keep her mind from the mountains and the dark; she would listen.

'In the Second War, I played no active part, needless to say. One-armed soldiers have small value. I was employed in a dubious section of the War Office, decoding messages.' His eyes, moist from drink, looked away to the distances of war. 'Sometimes, in that small and dusty room with blackout curtains at the window, I thought of those men who were struggling back, the way I had come, out of France over the passes into Spain — and myself not among them. In a way I was glad of the Blitz, for at least I was not free from all danger. And as the anti-aircraft barrage sounded outside, I remembered that time in Spain which seemed like the beginning, the time of Guernica and the Ebro, and the desolation of Barcelona . . .'

The sound of a distant telephone cut the silence, and Eve's head sharply turned, everything else for the moment forgotten. But no one came with news, and after a few minutes Benedict poured himself more whisky and said, 'If you would rather I stopped talking, I will.'

'No,' she said, 'I'd rather you talked.'

'After my wife died, I went more and more often, to Spain and Andorra. My path crossed with Carrie's some years ago; since then we've often met, as we both love Spain. For me, though I'm not a holy person, it's a holy place. Wasn't there a film long ago called *Blood and Sand*?'

'More than once,' Carrie said.

'Spain seems to me Blood and God. You find monasteries everywhere, and sometimes, though they are abandoned and desolate, you can feel the ashes of a fire of faith ... even some of its warmth.'

'Gosh,' said Bridget, 'that sounds kind of nice.'

Carrie said, 'I thought you didn't believe in relics and such?'

'Oh ... relics ... no, I don't really take to them. Nor do I go to church. But it really is impossible to live through a war in one's youth, and to come to be sixty, and not feel at times the whisper of things not seen. "The soul's dark cottage", perhaps.'

June said, 'Bridget and I go to church every Sunday. Not the same church, because Bridget's a Catholic and I'm Anglican — but we're both very ecumenical. We get laughed at sometimes, but we don't mind. As a nurse, Bridget has to see all kinds of suffering and death and grief; and as a social worker; I see a different kind, but quite a lot of it too.'

Bridget said, 'We prayed today for your son. We went to the Church of St Andrew, by the Casa del Vall.'

Carrie said, 'I go to *all* churches. Whatever they are. I've heard Mass in the strangest places. I got out of my sleeping-bag and went (dressed of course) to an early Mass once in Denia — Carthusians, I think they were. I don't doubt they were surprised to see me, but they took me in their stride. It was soon after my husband went away, and I was very unhappy: sorrow is a kind of entrance anywhere. But I am not unhappy now.'

The room was entirely quiet. Eve did not want these companionable voices to cease, for while they sounded she felt herself drawn into some larger place than the small contained cell of her own grief and fear: she felt at one with Carrie Morgan, and her life of travel, alone; with Benedict, who relived the old war and disasters of his youth; with Bridget and June, who might have been aggressively pious, but were not so, having a warmth, a selfless concern that transcended — or perhaps was the result of — their simplicity.

But when the voices stopped, she was at once aware of the lonely heights which surrounded the companionship of this place, and she exclaimed, half-rising from her chair, 'I must see if there's any news; I must see!'

Benedict put his one hand on her arm. 'I know you're waiting, and I know it's hell: waiting always is. But when you go through any such thing as you now endure, and have endured, you have one great gain: you tread a path that has been trodden so often before, but trodden to some purpose. Do you understand?'

She sat down. The doors to the kitchen swung, as a young waiter, yawning, came in and began to lay tables for breakfast. She said, 'Yes, I understand. Do they want us to go away?'

Benedict gave a casual glance at the young man, and poured more whisky. 'No one in Spain — or Andorra — wants one to do anything or not do anything. Non-politically speaking, that is. They talk all night in the *ramblas* of Barcelona, under your bedroom window. We could stay here till morning and no one would be at all surprised . . . The search won't make much headway in the dark. Start again at first light.'

How long before light? Apart from some distant drone of voices, the hotel seemed asleep. She saw Bridget yawn and said, 'You must all go to bed; you must be so tired.'

'No, we're not,' Bridget said. 'Speaking for myself, I'm used to night duty.'

'So'm I,' said Benedict, 'so long as there's enough booze.'

'And I,' said Carrie, 'have slept — or tried to sleep — so often in foreign parts, on my Lilo, that I've learned to make a friend of the night.'

Eve said sharply, 'Was that the telephone?'

'No; not yet.'

She did not look at her watch. It must be very late; the waiter had long gone, and the door to the kitchens swung no more. The telephone was quiet.

'You will find,' Benedict said, turning the liquid in his glass, 'that all places and all circumstances become possible after a time, and in some manner. There is nothing that one cannot finally endure——'

She said, 'I can't lose Nigel. Not now. I can't.'

'He will be found,' Carrie said.

'It's been too long.'

'You have to remember the shelters,' Benedict said. 'Sometimes no more than a wooden shrine, such as we passed on the road; sometimes a cattleman's hut. When we crossed into France, wounded men rested there. It was February then, and very cold. No light anywhere, just a world of great mountains and danger and snow. Unless they found shelter, the wounded had little chance. But there's no war or winter now.'

Quiet in the room deepened. 'Men go back to battlefields,' he said; 'I daresay they perceive some truth there which is absent from other places. Perhaps they feel that arenas of death are nearer to the heart of things than the plains of pleasure.' Draining his glass, he looked at Eve. 'Possibly, in the time since your husband's death, you've discovered the same thing? That the untroubled places, the playgrounds, are not the essential truth . . .'

Yes; she thought: that was so; but there was still the question——

Bridget said, 'Isn't it beginning to get light?'

Eve stared at the window. Certainly the colour beyond the transparent curtains had changed, not to light but to some greyness like a settling of dust, and the last of the candles paled.

Carrie put a hand on her arm. 'A little rest, I think: I'll come with you to your room. Then we'll return to the camp.'

The day had begun.

§

Quiet held the valley, and above this a sky of no colour. It seemed, in spite of the lessening dark, that the mist still drowned the heights. As she saw this she felt so sudden a fall of heart that she knew she had been living for some moments with hope.

Carrie glanced at her as she climbed into the car. 'Morning mist,' she said. 'There's warmth in the air: can't you feel it?'

'I don't know.'

Benedict stood with Bridget and June on the step. She glanced at them with a gratitude so profound that it could find no expression.

'We're going to wait here,' Bridget said. 'Like before. And Benedict——'

He made a shaky movement to the car. 'I'm coming with you. I've slept off the drink, and I want to be there.'

The car moved away from the hotel through the silent town. The shops were not yet open: the tawdry colours, the gleaming bottles were shut away; the road empty, but for themselves, of traffic. Now it was possible to see the town as it had once been: the ancient capital of the valley; a place of grey stone, with the Valira sending its urgent waters through on their way south.

She crouched in her seat, staring ahead, as the road twisted upward. Nothing but the steep mountainsides, grey with only the first brush strokes of colour. Slowly, as they climbed, the colour strengthened. She rubbed her eyes which were sandy with lack of sleep. Was there not also, within the colour, a brightness, a stronger light than she had seen since she had come to this place?

I mustn't hope too much, she thought . . . But out of the cloud of morning, little by little, detail bloomed in the first amber of day: a mass of boulders; far down the live skin of the river. Sun. Sun beginning to climb above the steep faces of the mountains, and send the long light of morning to dazzle the road ahead.

Benedict, whom she had thought to be asleep, said, 'The mist has gone. See? Quite gone. The weather's turned.'

Carrie, driving with her usual exhilarated speed, said with excitement, 'He was right — the rescue chap — the wind's changed. It's going to be hot.'

Perhaps this was true, for there was sweat on her forehead and palms. A change of wind . . . weather from the Mediterranean: warm winds and untrammelled sunlight.

In time?

The car climbed on, into the miracle of a different day. The white modern houses had the brilliance of the far snows. Villages were beginning to wake; women in black hung sheets from their balconies; here and there the light limned, as if with a craftsman's hand, the potted geraniums which hung from the windowsills. She could imagine, if she could not smell, the early morning essence of coffee and warm bread. A café beside the river, its shutters still closed against the sun, advertised *Truites par excellenzo*. Now a dazzle on the river, too bright for the eye to rest on.

'You see,' Carrie said, as the car swung and turned; 'it's summer.'

When they came to the camp, it was already soaked with light, as if there had indeed been some reversal of seasons. The number of people was greatly increased. Eve scrambled out of the car almost before it had stopped, and ran. The sun struck her shoulder like a heavy hand.

How many people were there, in this high valley? All about her she could hear the Catalan voices, the chatter of the boys. Some of the men seemed to be prepared for climbing — others waited, cigarettes in hand, like people at a railway station. She found Howard, his face already sweating from the open day. He said, 'You see . . . the wind's changed.'

Nothing more than this.

She asked, 'Yes, but what's happening?' for there seemed to be only confusion about her, many people moving in this new sun to no purpose.

Gene Carson joined them, with Mark close behind him. Gene said, 'They've called the *Centre de Vol en Montagne*. The helicopter's been standing by ever since Nigel was missing. Grounded by the weather. But now . . .'

They all looked upwards, but so far the amber-flushed peaks had the sky to themselves.

'A new rescue party's going out,' Gene said; 'the rest are waiting for a signal from the helicopter. In case it's impossible to land. We've got a whole lot of chaps . . . some rustled up from the *Vigurie Français*; some from the Spanish side . . . You can see that everything's being done.'

Yes, indeed; she could see that everything was being done: men, ropes, even a stretcher; the hope of the helicopter. Everything.

She could not know if it would be enough.

She sat on the rough ground and stared about her at the unclouded heights, at the benison of sun, at the activity about her. The long sleepless night was gone; she could see an image of the table with the candles burning low, the company which had sustained her, like the companions, ruffled, shiny and travel-stained, on a long journey. Carrie and Benedict were talking now in Spanish to a man from a rescue party.

She thought, I am not alone.

You have a future, Mrs Rutherford.

For the first time, she thought that if Nigel were found, it might be true.

If . . . she became aware that Mark was beside her. 'He's going to be all right, isn't he?' he asked. In the strong light he too looked as though he had slept little, his air of assurance gone.

She said at last, 'I hope so. We can't know.'

'Don't say that. He must be all right. I didn't say goodbye.'

She glanced up at him, for the words struck upon memory: of that last sight of Jamie, in the hall of the hotel, and his words, to which she had not replied. So nothing was new, and everything had an echo.

He said, 'It was warm last night. And today . . .'

She nodded, still held within the strangeness of pattern, of loss, of hope. About to speak, she heard a voice call in some foreign lan-

136

guage: she saw the stir amongst the men who stood there. Then she heard the sound.

It was not, she thought, the same sound as an aircraft; it rang through the valleys and peaks like a drill.

The voices exclaimed; they all looked up, shading their eyes. Like the shepherds, she thought, in childhood pictures, who looked to the star. The ungainly yet beautiful thing came into view, bringing hope, sweeping over the sky with a spinning blur of its rotor blades. Its bright yellow fuselage dazzled in the sun.

Eve, like the rest, looked upward. Inquisitive, tireless, the noisy craft, having the aspect of a huge wasp, dipped and turned, searching and searching from the sky.

She said to Gene Carson who stood near her, 'What will they do if they see him and can't land?'

'Radio through to the guys here and tell them where he is. That one with the black curls and the green jacket — one of the French party — he's all ready to receive the message.'

She looked at the dark Frenchman, who could give her news of life or death. He stood with the radio receiver in his hand, speaking casually to the man at his side. The French was rapid, too fast to understand. She thought, as she had before at Rosthwaite, that this was the easiest time, with the penetrating noise from the sky, the polyglot voices about her, the ease brought by Carrie and Benedict, the sunlight and the hope of rescue. But if rescue failed, these people would all disperse, and she would have to return home.

I wouldn't know what to do, she thought; I truly wouldn't know. She kept her eyes on the helicopter which turned and twisted, as if it performed some acrobatic for their benefit. The noise covered them all, a wide umbrella of sound.

Larry Howard stood beside her, as if he wished to find words of comfort. He said, 'Know anything about helicopters?'

She shook her head.

'That's a French one. *Alouette*. Means a lark; expect you know that. Used to be very interested in them — helicopters, that is: see the small rotor blades on the tail? They keep the whole thing from going sideways, if you get what I mean.' He gave her a swift glance, perhaps to see whether she understood that this was the only way he could express his concern. 'Damned difficult business, piloting one of those things. Need to have the skill of a horseman — be part of the machine, as it were——'

He broke off as the radio crackled loudly; she saw the Frenchman hold the receiver to his ear; Luis Madero called 'Silencio! Wait. I think is news——'

Eve sat still. All of them were suddenly quiet, and the only sounds were the turning blades of the helicopter and the crackle of voices on the radio, distorted, incomprehensible. A halt in time, in the long wait. Again a clear memory of Borrowdale and Sarah coming alone towards the hotel through the rain . . .

Carrie and Benedict were beside her. None of them spoke; all looked at the yellow gleaming craft in the sky, while the mechanised foreign voices echoed in the rock-bound valley.

Then Luis ran towards her. He had a look of exhausted triumph. 'Señora! They have seen him! He has been distinguished——'

She felt a hand, perhaps Carrie's, on her shoulder. Hope and fear kept her for a moment silent. Then she said, 'Is he alive?'

'I believe, Señora. I believe he has moved——'

This tremendous hope, turbulent, like the vibration of the machine above them. She said, 'Moved?'

'He has done so . . .' He lifted one arm, as if in greeting.

As he did so, she caught sight of Mark's face as he listened: strained with hope, even with love . . .

She said, 'What will they do?'

Howard said, his voice enthusiastic with knowledge, 'If they can't land, they'll maybe let down a winch-man with a harness, and he'll bring Nigel up, into the helicopter. You'll have seen something like it on television perhaps——'

She was on her feet, staring upwards, where her hope lay. The shining yellow machine hung high, the blur of its propellers a misty circle. For a moment nothing happened; then the side of the helicopter slid open, and the figure of a man in helmet and rough jacket crawled out. He swung, as the wire which held him like an umbilical cord let him further and further down . . .

Now they could see nothing, for the winch-man was out of sight within the folded hillsides, and there was only the powerful thing in the sky, able to hover, move sideways and backwards with extreme skill.

Then slowly the winch swung. Slowly upwards. Too far away to see more than the man with his helmet, and the smaller figure in a harness, like a cradle, being drawn up from the place where he'd been found.

138

The winch swung, with its burden.

She heard a voice exclaim in a foreign tongue; she said urgently to Benedict, 'I didn't understand — what did he say?'

Benedict said, 'He saw the boy move.'

Too much to take in; too much to believe.

Yet, perhaps, impossible not to believe it.

The winch shortened in the dazzling air; it might have been some escapade, performed as before for their entertainment. Except that . . .

Up and up, until the open side of the helicopter received them, like kindness, like mercy, like the end of fear.

But she couldn't yet know.

Now, the wound in its side closed, the machine moved again; again she heard the crackle of the radio transmitter, and the Frenchman called to them, making movements with his arms.

Benedict said, 'She's going to land here. There is space, where the camp is. But we have to get out of the way — there's a great down-draught of air from the rotor-blades.'

She stood back with the rest of them. The cleared ground did not seem to her large enough for anything to land on. Benedict beside her, perhaps catching her thought, said, 'They can land on a pinhead. Knew a chap who flew them: you have to keep your mind on three things at once, if not more.'

Now the shining thing, with a dragon's roar, was immediately above them, growing larger as it came to land. The down-draught whipped at their hair, at their eyes, at their clothes, so that they stood, teeth clenched, like people in the face of a storm. She was glad of the noise and the whipping of the air, since they seemed to stun thought. As the machine slid downwards, she saw the rough grass pouring away in the rush of air . . . what were the words in her mind? An angel that troubled the waters . . .

At once, as the machine landed she made to move forward, but Benedict's hand held her back. 'Wait for the rotor blades to stop.'

Obedient, she waited. The propellers spun slower, more slowly, till from a blurred circle they became separate blades, turning like a slowed top.

Now the door slid back and now they were all running forward, a mesh of voices taking the place of the machine's sound. For a moment she stood still, the impulse to move overcome by fear.

It was done now. The operation was successful; the multiplied skills of the rescue teams and the helicopter pilot and the winch-man had brought Nigel from the lost and lonely place where he must have spent three nights on the mountain.

But now there was nothing to divert her; no dazzling yellow bird drilling its noise in the sky; no performance of daring and excitement: only the certainty, like the certainty which comes at the end of a journey to a place of which one is afraid.

Carrie took her arm. She moved forward, amongst the many voices, aware of nothing now save the growing heat of the sun, and the young man who climbed from the machine. Now she could see Nigel, for they were handing him down, a slight, slack body, it seemed to her, and she said, 'Oh please ... please ...' though whom she pleaded with, she didn't know.

She heard Carrie say, 'Look! It's all right!'; and Eve ran forward.

She stood, looking down at her son. So far off, in such a different day, she had looked at Jamie's face, in death, in the grey mists of Borrowdale. But she was aware of Jamie, not as he had been in death, but his voice sounding with its upward cheerfulness: loud and part of life ...

Nigel lay on a stretcher on the rough ground. He was dirtied, dishevelled, his skin pale, the eyes dark-ringed; his hair matted with mud and sweat. But he moved his head and opened his eyes. '*Ma*? ... And a helicopter ... Ma, they found me. I've been in a helicopter.'

Life, she thought. She said nothing, merely smiled at him, knowing she must not weep.

Now the doctor from the rescue team spoke indecipherable words and explored Nigel's body; gently touched the foot. When Nigel grimaced with pain, he said in English, 'I will put on bandage — dipped in the stream — it will become plaster of paris; it is like magic, no?' The man spoke further in his own tongue. Nigel had closed his eyes again; the pallor of his skin had intensified, his face looked shadowed and thin.

She said, 'Nigel——' but Benedict turned to her. 'No cause for alarm. He's exhausted and cold, but not dangerously so. Most likely a bone broken in the foot: painful, but not serious. All he needs is rest and warmth and food.'

She knelt down beside him. Perhaps nothing had been so good as this warm ground, and Nigel's face, regaining colour, turned to her, his eyes open. 'I don't know what you're doing her, Ma; it's all very odd.' He closed his eyes, and might have slept.

Eve sat back on her heels with her forehead in her hands. Voices converged about her: plans were being made: dimly she heard that they would take Nigel by jeep to the hotel, and she would go with him and there he would rest before being flown back to England ... Yes, all this would happen, and she would be part of it, but for the moment she was stupefied with relief, with gratitude, with something larger than both of these, perhaps humility and awe, aware of forces beyond knowledge and sight.

For in Nigel's recovery there seemed for the first time a flow of warmth, as if the icy stone of misery had begun to ease and melt. As if Jamie, who was lost, whose voice could not be heard again, was not altogether lost, had still some power.

She looked with joy and exhaustion at Benedict and Carrie who stood near her. She said, 'I'm so grateful ... for last night. For ...' She ran out of words. The men of the rescue team, the pilot of the helicopter, Howard and Carson, the boys (including Mark) had all been part of this. It was a gift, a wave of comfort and goodwill. Somewhere in this high place, in the hot sun, with Nigel lamed and weak but alive, there was blessing, the first of ease.

10

The train slid past the bronze and iron of this English Autumn afternoon. Contrast with that last sight of Andorra, with its southern heat, was extreme. Heat and cloudless skies had endured until she and Nigel had left, on a flight from Barcelona over a sunstripped country when, with the Channel and the English coast, the clouds came and the airport was shiny with rain.

Now the day was dry, without sun. Another journey; yet with a difference. She glanced at Nigel who sat opposite her. His eyes closed with the murmur and swing of the train, and she was able to observe him.

Certainly he looked older; his face still wanted flesh, the eyes still bruised with shadow. His foot was out of plaster, and he had a stick beside him. Though he grumbled about it, she thought he had a certain pride in using it as he limped. Yes; older, nearer to a man and further from a boy. She could see Jamie there more clearly than before, not only in face, but in set of shoulder, in movement.

Brilliant as a picture lighted for especial attention that moment of rescue in the hot sun would return like a talisman. She recalled Mark's words about the quarrel, and her own conclusions that if you built badly, worse must follow.

But perhaps that was not quite true? Perhaps though in the haze of darkness and pain you chose wrongly, behaved with the confusion of one not in her right mind, the end was better than you could believe; mercy given you, though you seemed to deserve none.

It appeared so. It appeared so now.

A taxi took them to the vicarage, which as always seemed to stand sunless within its heavy trees. Nigel, leaning on his stick, looked about him with interest. '*Ages* since I've been here.'

'You usen't to care for it much.'

'No ... but I rather do now. Norfolk isn't like anything else, quite, is it? Oh, there's the swing: I remember that.'

It hung, lopsided, unused, below the bronze trees, speaking of lost childhood.

Mrs Bussy, the woman from the village, opened the door to them. With Nigel limping on his stick, she led them into the large sitting-room.

Nigel said, 'Hullo, Grandfather.'

The old man rose slowly, with a pressure of hands on his chair.

'So there's the young man who came near to perishing in the Pyrenees! Let's see what it's done to you.'

Nigel made a face. 'Only my foot. I'm afraid I caused an awful lot of bother.'

The old man gave an amused, dry smile. Though it was not long since she had seen him, Eve could remark a change in him. The lean face was leaner, the hands shook. Yet she could see also the pleasure in his face, the contained joy of a man not used to showing his feelings, at the sight of his grandson.

'Come and sit down,' he said, as Nigel limped across the room. 'Sit near me, as like a lot of old people I don't always hear so very well. Sorry I couldn't meet you at the station, but some sort of bug invaded my bronchial tubes . . . How tedious much of old age is!' He leant back in his chair with an abrupt gasp of relief and looked at Nigel who sat on a stool beside him, his stick on the floor and his leg stretched out. The tired eyes had light in them as he examined the boy at his feet.

'So you spent three nights on a mountain in Andorra and got rescued by helicopter! D'you feel proud of it?'

'Well — not really. It just seems rather odd. Especially now I'm home.'

'Not proud of being the centre of newspaper comment, head-lines; not to mention interviews with Headmasters on television? I think I would have been, at your age.'

Nigel looked down at his stick. 'Perhaps I was a bit when I saw the press cuttings: Mark's parents sent them to me. I had to send them back, because Mark's mother shows them to everyone and says, "Mark was there, you know." Bit shaming really.'

'Ah, yes; your friend Mark.'

'D'you know he tried to come and look for me? Terribly odd, because it wasn't his thing at all.'

'Well, of course, as you'll learn, people do act out of character, particularly under stress.'

Eve sat silent, grateful to be so. The room was darkening and Clyde Rutherford switched on a table-lamp beside him. This put him and his grandson in a pool of light which emphasised the youth of Nigel's face, and the age of Clyde's. Outside, the bronze day was drifting into a haze of autumnal mist, as if the garden drowned in smoke. She only just heard their voices, for the confrontation between them, with the absent third, sent her thoughts into another dimension: there was mystery in the two who faced each other, the old man and the boy; the mystery of age and youth, of their life and Jamie quiet in death.

Their voices returned to her. 'Were you frightened?' Clyde was saying.

'Oh, yes. Until I found the hut. I couldn't believe the hut at first. And then I thought it was the one I'd seen before, but of course it wasn't. I wondered if the cow-herd or someone would come back, but the place seemed deserted; he must have left for the winter. I kept telling myself that the rest must be looking for me. There was straw and some food ... I got sleepy and kind of dozed; I don't know how long. The pain in my foot kept waking me up. I shivered a lot; it was like having a temperature. And when I thought of the mountains outside, the high ones with snow on them, I *was* scared, because it was like being lost in an enormous place, how you are sometimes in dreams. Once I tried to get out of the shelter, but the mist was so thick and I didn't know which way to go, and I remembered that cold was the most dangerous thing, so I stayed where I was.'

'That,' Clyde said, knocking his pipe against the grate, 'in all probability saved your life.' Did he, Eve wondered, think of Jamie, who had not life any more? 'What happened next?'

'I can't quite remember. Time got blurred. Once I thought I heard a voice calling, but it was a long way off and though I tried to call back I couldn't make enough noise. The voice went away. I think I was frightened then; I wondered if anyone would ever come.'

'But they did.'

'Oh, yes. Suddenly there was all this sun; it was like magic. And when I first heard the noise I thought it was an avalanche — I was a bit dopey, I suppose; but it went on, coming nearer and then fading, circling. And I crawled out of the shelter, because I was afraid the helicopter wouldn't see me, and they'd go away, like the voice did. I managed to get my anorak off, and waved it. Then I saw this man coming out of the sky. And when he pulled me up into the helicopter it was like flying over the mountains. Pretty terrific.'

Eve sat, still silent, her eyes on the old man's face as he listened. What did she read there? A recognition of the unknown future, of his own death perhaps, and the long years of Nigel's life, which he would not see.

Clyde said, 'So you came home. Would you go on such an endeavour again?'

Nigel seemed to think about it. Nearly seventeen, Eve thought; not a boy any more: he would make his own decisions, turn to distant adventures, love, perhaps climb, like Jamie; travel a path of which she could rightly have no knowledge.

'Yes, I think so,' he said. 'I loved the mountains. And that time in the hut — of course it was hell for everybody, but for me — would it be awfully pompous to say it was important?'

Clyde shook his head. 'You could say that any experience of adversity is important.'

Eve looked aside to the window. The words, though simple, came to her with force. Their voices went on, but she saw the ghostly garden, where the swing was barely discernible and the trees hung in the hush of the oncoming dark. Important? Perhaps these months since Jamie's death had not been fruitless; had even brought gain.

She heard Clyde say, 'You usen't to like this place very much. I remember once you fell out of the swing and yelled loudly till you were taken home.'

'I was only a kid. I like it now. Ma said you'd been ill. Really ill?'

A dry smile. 'I don't know what "really ill" is. The machine wears out, I suppose——'

Eve interrupted. 'Has Valerie Vaughan been to see you?'

The smile was turned on her. 'Oh — once or twice. But she's going to be married, you know; a widower, some years younger than me. So old age must be as it is . . . Listen!'

Eve looked up. Clyde said, 'Bell-ringing. Begins now and lasts for an hour. (You remember, Eve?) Some people complain, but *I* like it, so it goes on. Eve, open the window a little; you seem to be the most mobile of the three of us.'

She went to the window and thrust at the pane. As it lifted, the tumble of sound came with greater strength, part of the moist autumnal air speaking of mystery across the fields.

For some moments they were silent as if the sound cast a spell. Eve stood by the window, looking into the dusk. The sound had a quality which spoke of old things, of childhood, of love and

Jamie, and birth and death, and the unknown territory beyond either.

'They toil hard,' Clyde said, 'people from the village — then when they've finished they go to the pub: it's thirsty work.'

The sound and the air flowed into the room. Outside she could see a little square of light in the dissolving garden. Pale as dust, a few late roses showed on the dark, and she remembered the walk with Rufus Stevens on a summer evening.

That was past. Now, tenuously, with hope, not empty of fear, she held on to something new.

Clyde said, 'That's enough; the room's getting cold.'

She shut the window. Though diminished the bells still faintly sounded, as if they spoke to her.